Narrow Walk

by Shirley Brinkerhoff

FOCUS ON THE FAMILY

PUBLISHING
Colorado Springs, Colorado

NARROW WALK

Library of Congress Cataloging-in-Publication Data

Brinkerhoff, Shirley.
   Narrow walk/Shirley Brinkerhoff.
      p. cm.—(The Nikki Sheridan series: #3)
   Summary: While visiting Southern California with her aunt, Nikki's
newly acquired Christian faith is tested by an illegal alien who seems to be
involved in drug smuggling, and an arrogant girl who looks down on every-
thing Nikki does.
   ISBN 1-56179-539-9
   [1. Christian life—Fiction. 2. Drug traffic—Fiction. 3. Illegal aliens—
Fiction. 4. Aunts—Fiction. 5. California—Fiction.] I. Title. II. Series:
Brinkerhoff, Shirley. Nikki Sheridan series; 3.
PZ7.B780115Nar   1997   97-24439
[Fic]—dc21   CIP
                                            AC

Published by Focus on the Family Publishing,
Colorado Springs, Colorado 80995

This is a work of fiction, and any resemblance between the characters in this
book and real persons is coincidental.

Scripture quotations are from *The Holy Bible, New International Version*
(NIV) © 1973, 1984 by International Bible Society, used by permission of
Zondervan Publishing House.

Focus on the Family books are available at special quantity discounts when
purchased in bulk by corporations, organizations, churches, or groups. Special
imprints, messages, and excerpts can be produced to meet your needs. For
more information, write: Special Sales, Focus on the Family Publishing, 8605
Explorer Drive, Colorado Springs, CO 80920, or call (719) 531-3400 and ask
for the Special Sales Department.

Cover Design: Candi L. D'Agnese
Cover Illustration: Cheri Bladholm

Printed in the United States of America

97 98 99 00/10 9 8 7 6 5 4 3 2 1

To Patti,
who is always there when it matters most.
1 Samuel 23:16

❧ *One* ❧

EVERYTHING WOULD BE DIFFERENT now that she was a Christian.

Nikki Sheridan was totally sure of that.

She fidgeted a little in her seat, sitting sandwiched between Aunt Marta on her right and the little white-haired woman on her left who'd been snoring softly for the entire four-hour flight, ever since they left the runway at Grand Rapids.

This two-week trip to California might look like just a vacation to everyone else, but in Nikki's mind, it was a chance to start all over again. She would finally—*finally*—quit messing things up the way she had this past year. And best of all, nobody here had to even know what was in her past.

Her right foot, asleep from all that sitting, began to prickle as though needles were jabbing the bottom of it. She would have to get up and move around. Nikki slowly unfolded her stiff body and got cautiously to her feet in the narrow space. She grasped the back of the blue upholstered seat in front of her with one hand and tried to balance her clear plastic cup of

7-Up in the other. Just then, the plane lurched, dropping far enough and fast enough that Nikki winced at the unbearable pressure in her ears and the sick sensation in her stomach.

Even worse, her 7-Up seemed to have developed a mind of its own, and she watched in horror as it splashed over the rim of the plastic cup, cascading down the back of the man who sat in front of her, turning the denim of his shirt dark-blue where the liquid soaked in.

The plane steadied itself almost immediately, and the calm, reassuring voice of the pilot sounded from the speakers overhead.

"Well, there you go, ladies and gentlemen—a little bonus excitement for you. At no extra charge. You can get that kind of service only from United."

Twitters of nervous laughter erupted here and there throughout the plane, then an almost palpable feeling of relief took over as the pilot continued.

"Seriously, folks, that was just a little . . ."

But Nikki never did hear his explanation. There in row 22, the pilot's words were drowned out by the sound of her own voice babbling apologies to the passenger she'd just baptized with soda. He jerked upright when the ice-cold 7-Up doused his back, then whirled around in his seat to face her, black brows drawn together over dark-blue eyes.

"I didn't mean to do that!" she cried, words spilling out in a jumbled rush as she leaned over the seat and grabbed for her cup, which had fallen between his back and the seat back. "I mean, it wasn't my fault! I was just trying to get to the rest room before the 'fasten seat belts' sign came on, and right at the minute I stood up, the plane—"

Wait a minute, said a voice inside her head. *Isn't this the way you used to react, always blaming and making excuses? Before you became a Christian?*

Nikki stopped dead.

The man worked his shoulders back and forth a few times inside his shirt, trying to unstick the cold, wet denim from the skin of his back, and the whole time he did, his blue eyes never left her face.

Nikki gulped and made a tough decision—she would listen to the voice inside, despite her embarrassment. She took a deep breath and began again, more slowly.

"I'm really sorry," she said, noting the open denim shirt over a white T-shirt and chinos. *This guy is incredibly good-looking,* she realized suddenly, and a line from the old song her grandmother sometimes sang popped into her head: "You oughta be in pictures." Nikki felt her cheeks begin to flush. *Wouldn't you know I'd pick the best-looking guy on the plane to do this to?*

She glanced away. Not even five minutes ago, gazing out the double-paned plane window at the green hills below, she'd been ecstatic about how wonderful two whole weeks in Southern California were going to be—and in April, when summer was still pretty much a dream back in Michigan! But now . . .

I haven't even gotten off the plane, and I'm already screwing things up.

From seat 22C beside her came a muffled snort, and Nikki looked down at Aunt Marta, who sat with one elbow on her tray table, head leaning into her hand. The shoulders of her rust-colored jacket shook as she tried to hold back her laughter. Even the ends of her gray-streaked blonde hair, twisted up into the usual haphazard knot at the back of her head, trembled.

Then, to make things worse, a flight attendant who had obviously seen Nikki's entire performance—a graceful, pencil-slim blonde who would never be so clumsy as to spill soda down somebody's back—hurried down the aisle with a handful of napkins and began dabbing at the man's wet shirt.

Nikki sighed. *Could we make this any more obvious? Why don't we just get the pilot to announce the whole thing over the loudspeaker? "Klutz from Michigan soaks California movie star (or look-alike) with ice-cold 7-UP."*

"Look, I'm really, really sorry," Nikki began again, but the man waved her words away with a nonchalant hand, suddenly charming as the lovely flight attendant leaned closer to him. She was surprised to see the skin around his eyes crinkle as his face relaxed into an easy smile. His teeth were amazingly white and straight in that tanned face.

"Don't worry about it," he said. "The way the plane dropped like that, I know you couldn't help it. I'm just glad it wasn't tomato juice."

The flight attendant added her apologies about the plane's erratic behavior. Aunt Marta finally got hold of herself and looked up with a straight face, and Nikki, after mumbling a few more apologies, escaped to one of the tiny, stuffy rest rooms at the rear of the plane. She shut the door behind her and leaned against it with another long sigh.

She stayed in the rest room long enough for the blush to fade from her cheeks, giving her time to fix her hair and control the curls that were running wild in the dry air of the plane. With the tip of her index finger, she smoothed lip gloss across her pale lips, then brushed away a dried scrap of mascara from underneath one eye. She took another deep breath and started back to her seat, twisting sideways to squeeze past the line of people waiting for the rest room.

By the time she got back to row 22, Aunt Marta and the dark-haired man were deep in conversation. Marta was leaning forward, talking animatedly, and when she stood to let Nikki pass, she spoke to her niece with excitement.

"Guess what, Nikki! This is Lee Tierney. He teaches biology at South State University, where we're going. He's on his way back from Mexico, from another interdisciplinary conference—just like the one Alex and I are chairing here next week—and last month he was at one in Central America." She turned back to Lee. "This is my niece, Nicole Sheridan. I brought her along partly to help Alex and me with office work these next few days while we get things ready for the conference, and partly to have a vacation."

Nikki squeezed past her aunt and slid back into the middle seat as Marta and Lee Tierney compared notes. She remembered her aunt telling her about Alex. That was Dr. Alexandra Fortenay, sociology professor at South State and co-chair with Marta of the conference, but the rest of the names they mentioned meant nothing to her. Still, she found herself listening in because Marta, normally so levelheaded, seemed unusually animated in the presence of this professor.

So maybe I'm not the only one who noticed how good-looking this guy is, Nikki thought.

Anxious to be free of the small, confining seat, she was glad when the plane at last began its slow descent. The seat belt signs finally lit up, and she knew it wouldn't be long until they landed at the Santa Linnea airport.

The blonde flight attendant took her final stroll up the aisle, noting in a bored tone the tray tables still down and seats still reclined—bored, that was, until she reached row 21, where Lee Tierney sat. Then her voice turned especially charming.

"I'm sorry, but I'll have to ask you to put your seat back into its upright position, sir."

Nikki could hear the smile in Lee Tierney's voice when he answered.

"For you? No problem!" He spoke back over his shoulder to Marta once more before adjusting his seat. "My car's at the airport, and I'm driving right out to my office on campus. May I offer you a ride?"

Marta hesitated a fraction of a second. "Thank you, but a friend of mine is meeting us. It's very kind of you to offer, though."

Nikki glanced sideways at her aunt. She knew Marta was referring to Ted Wilcox, a college friend who was now pastor of a small church outside Santa Linnea. There had been a special warmth in her voice when she told Nikki about him the week before.

But now, Nikki thought, *she sounds almost sorry Ted's coming.*

❧ Two ❧

AS MARTA AND NIKKI SQUEEZED out of their seats, Lee motioned them ahead of him. They threaded their way off the plane and through the small airport to the baggage carousel, where Lee helped them retrieve their luggage. As soon as they tried to leave the baggage area, however, it became apparent there was a problem. Passengers were lining up at the exit, anxious to be on their way, but something was stopping them.

"What's going on?" Nikki asked finally, nudging her wheeled suitcase ahead with her foot and shifting her heavy carry-on from one hand to the other.

Marta stood on tiptoe, craning her neck to see over the people in front of her, then shook her head. "I don't know. I can't see anything."

Lee spoke from just behind them. "Probably another suitcase raid," he said with a bite of sarcasm in his voice.

Both Marta and Nikki turned around to stare at him, and Nikki noticed how far up she had to look to meet those blue eyes.

"Suitcase raid?" she asked, thinking about all the new underwear she'd shoved into her suitcase at the last minute, right on top. She'd never anticipated anyone looking inside. She anxiously scanned the crowd around her, wondering which of these people would see what her grandmother still referred to as "unmentionables."

Lee smiled down at her. "Well, that's what the people who live here call them. Santa Linnea's had more than its usual share of drug problems these last few months, and the police are determined to find out how the stuff's getting into town. Every few days now, they pick a flight and search luggage at random." He crossed his arms in front of him, tapping one elbow with his hand. His fingers were long and slender and as tanned as his face, and they tapped in a slow, even arc against the fabric of his denim shirt.

"Oh, brother," Nikki groaned. "I hope they don't open *my* suitcase in front of everybody."

Lee gave a short laugh. "I wouldn't worry if I were you, Nikki. You don't look like a very good drug-smuggling prospect to me. I think they just pick on people who come from places where they know there's a lot of drug traffic."

It was another 10 minutes before they were waved to the head of the line.

"Ted's probably wondering what on earth is taking us so long," Marta said in a low voice to her niece. "I told him to just meet us out in front."

Ahead of them were three uniformed policemen standing beside a long table where they set the suitcases to be searched. Nikki gave a sigh of relief as one of the men motioned her on. But her relief changed when the same policeman reached down and wrestled Marta's bulging brown leather suitcase to the table with a thump.

Oh, no. Nikki cringed. She was well aware of her aunt's sloppy packing style. If there was anything worse than having her own suitcase inspected, it was having them search Marta's. *And in front of Lee, no less!* Nikki thought.

The policeman tugged at the zipper, which appeared to be stuck. He frowned and got a better grip, then pulled hard.

"Lady—I don't know—what you've got in—here!" he said, his words coming out unevenly as he worked.

Marta bit at her lower lip and didn't answer.

The policeman forced the zipper open the last few inches, and the suitcase lid sprang up on its own, as though opening was a relief. Marta's clothes, squashed into much too small a space, bulged over the edges.

Now it was Nikki's turn to laugh, and she avoided looking at Marta's face, knowing she'd lose it completely if their eyes met. From past experience she knew that Marta, meticulous to a fault about her research and writing as a musicologist, or about the elaborate gourmet menus she loved to concoct in the kitchen, had no patience at all with mundane tasks such as filling a suitcase.

Nikki had watched her often, packing to leave after a visit to her parents' blue clapboard house on the shore of Lake Michigan. Marta always forced herself, tight-lipped, to fold the first few garments precisely. As she went on, the folding grew more and more haphazard until she finally ended up tossing clothes in helter-skelter, wedging in last-minute additions around the sides, then leaning on the bulging top, her weight maneuvering it into a position where she could force the zipper shut.

Marta looked down at the jumble of clothes with dismay

and said, to no one in particular, "Those baggage handlers must really throw these suitcases around for things to get so messed up."

Nikki couldn't contain her laughter any longer, but Lee Tierney nodded gravely as though what Marta said made perfect sense to him.

"Isn't that the truth," he agreed.

"Marta! Marta! Hi!"

A man was waving from the other side of the baggage area. Smiling broadly, he walked swiftly to the table where Marta's luggage was being examined, and Nikki realized he must be Ted.

When Marta introduced Nikki, Ted's smile extended to her also. But when Lee was introduced, Ted's smile faded immediately.

The professor looked down at Ted, who was at least a head shorter, and extended his hand. Ted shook it, but as Nikki watched them together, she thought how totally different they were. Where Lee Tierney was tall and his dark good looks naturally drew every eye in his direction, Ted Wilcox was someone you'd never notice in a crowd. There was an intensity about Lee, those blue eyes seeming to look right through you and take charge of every situation. Ted, on the other hand, with his mild brown eyes and relaxed manner, looked content to go with the flow.

Then, too, Nikki thought, *being bald on top doesn't help much, either.*

Ted's bushy eyebrows and the sparse fringe growing around the back of his head in a half circle from ear to ear were the only hair he could boast, and even that was the same unremarkable brown as his eyes.

She watched Marta glance back and forth between the two men as she introduced them and wondered if her aunt was mentally racking up the contrasts, too.

Ted acknowledged the introduction by saying, "I suppose you could say that Lee and I already know each other."

And he doesn't sound at all happy about it, Nikki thought. Was it possible that Ted was jealous? Even though Aunt Marta was 10 years younger than her own mother, Nikki had always simply classified her as "old." The idea that men could be interested in her, possibly even jealous over her, was an eye-opener. She watched with new interest to see what would happen next.

Lee raised his eyebrows briefly at Ted's comment. "Oh, yes. Aren't you the preacher at that church south of town? That little white one beside the banana field?" He gave a sardonic smile, almost as though he was challenging Ted to say more.

Instead, the policeman cleared his throat and interrupted. "Look, lady, everything inside here seems to be okay, but I'm gonna have to ask you to close this thing up." He nodded toward the suitcase, where the brown leather top rested a good six inches above the bottom half, and his expression clearly read, *This I can't wait to see!* He cleared his throat again. "I'm not exactly sure how you got it zipped in the first place."

Both Ted and Lee came to Marta's aid immediately, squashing down opposite sides of the top so that, slowly and painstakingly, Marta was able to inch the zipper shut. When she finished, she looked up triumphantly at the policeman, who shook his head back and forth slightly as though he didn't quite believe his eyes.

As they filed through the exit gate of the baggage area, Marta said to Nikki in a low voice that only she could hear, "How about I hire you to do my packing next time?"

Just before they went their separate ways in the airport lobby, Lee asked, "Sure about that ride, Marta?"

"Yes, I'm sure," Marta answered. "Ted's dropping us off at the car rental place, so we'll be fine."

"Well, don't forget my offer to show you around. Santa Linnea's a charming town, especially if you see it with someone who knows the out-of-the-way places." Lee cocked his head a little to one side and flashed his white-toothed smile at Marta.

She glanced sideways at Ted, who was watching her face intently, before she answered Lee. "Well, I don't know how much free time I'll have since Dr. Fortenay and I are directing the conference this year, but thanks for the offer. I'm sure I'll see you there."

Lee dipped his head toward Ted, winked at Nikki, and said, "Next time, hang on to that soda a little tighter," then turned and left.

"What was that all about?" Ted asked.

Nikki shook her head, embarrassed, and it was Marta who answered with a grin. "I think you had to be there to get the full effect, Ted. Nikki soaked the professor with 7-Up when the plane took a sudden drop."

Ted looked at Nikki and grinned. His brown eyes were kind, and she felt suddenly that he remembered precisely how it felt to be 17.

❦ *Three* ❦

THE CAR RENTAL AGENCY didn't exactly live up to its advertisement of "Service in Five Minutes," but Marta had the keys in hand in less than 30. Ted stood in line with them while they waited, getting to know Nikki better and setting up times when he could see Marta.

"The weather's supposed to be great midweek, so we could get some sailing in then," he said.

"You have a sailboat?" Nikki asked, thinking that Ted didn't fit her idea of a sailor.

"Not only does he have one, sweetie," Marta laughed, "he *lives* on it."

"You're kidding." Nikki looked at Ted with surprise.

"Nope. She's not," he said. "It's not a yacht or anything fancy. I wouldn't want you to get the wrong idea. It's just a little 36-foot sloop I call *Wind Dancer*. She's right down in the harbor, any time you want to visit. So, Marta, when's your first free evening?"

Marta hesitated. "I'm not sure, Ted. Things are different

this year since Alex and I are actually running the conference instead of just attending. How about if I let you know?"

She glanced at her watch pointedly, and Ted nodded.

The sun was beginning to set as they left the car rental agency in a red Grand Am. Nikki looked around the black interior and sniffed the new car smell with appreciation.

"You know, this is a really nice car!"

Marta grinned. "And if you're really good, I just might let you drive it! Actually, you'll probably get to drive it more than I do. Alex passes our hotel on her way to the university, and she said she'd be glad to pick me up. I imagine that some days you'll want to sleep late or go sight-seeing, so I'll just leave the car for you."

As she listened, Nikki stared at the countryside, so foreign-looking, so different from Michigan. They rounded a sharp bend at the end of the airport drive, and across the street a cluster of tiny, run-down houses came into view.

"Look at those, Aunt Marta. They're practically shacks. You think anyone really lives there?"

Only the faintest hint of the paint they'd once worn remained, faded and peeling off the wooden siding, and the few porches still intact sloped dangerously in one direction or the other.

"I'm afraid so," Marta answered. "The immigrant situation is a pretty big problem out here, and sometimes they end up in places like that."

They turned another corner, and the ocean came into view, framed by palm trees.

"Look at that!" Nikki cried. "Do you realize this is the first time I've ever seen the Pacific?"

"Well, prepare to see it up close. The hotel's right on the ocean, and so is the university. Speaking of which, do you mind if we drop by the campus before we go to the hotel?" Marta asked. "I need to check in with Alex and make sure everything's going according to schedule. That way, you can get to meet her, too."

"That's fine," Nikki answered, watching the palm trees silhouetted against the coral-colored sunset. "Is she the one I'll actually be working with?"

"No, you'll be working with her daughter, MacKenzie," Marta said, braking to a stop at a red light. "She works at the university, too—I think in the registrar's office—and I know she does most of the paperwork for the conference. There's a lot of it. Maybe MacKenzie will be around tonight, and you can meet her, too."

"I'd like that. You said she's a student at the university, right? Do you know what year?"

"She's a freshman, not too much older than you, Nikki." Marta glanced over at her niece and shook her head.

Nikki knew what was coming next and recited in a quick singsong to head it off. "I know, I know. You just can't believe I'm this old already. Why, you can remember when I was just knee high to a grasshopper—"

Marta reached out and swatted playfully at the air beside Nikki's knee. "All right. You got me. I was actually going to say it again."

"I felt it coming," Nikki said. "I'll forgive you this one more time—as long as you promise not to say things like that in front of other people, okay?" When Marta didn't answer,

Nikki continued. "Actually, I don't think your mind's on what I'm saying at all. I think you're seeing visions of Lee Tierney, the incredible professor. Or . . . let's see." Nikki struck a pose with her chin on one hand and a dreamy look in her eyes. "Could it be Ted, the handsome sailor? Well, maybe not handsome, but Ted the sailor."

"*Nikki!*" Marta's expression was halfway between laughing and irritation. "Ted is a good friend—one of my best friends, in fact. And that's *all*. And his looks don't have anything to do with it." She braked for another stoplight, then made a right turn in front of a low brick wall with the words South State University on it. "You understand?"

"Right," Nikki answered, grinning. "I just don't think that's how Ted feels." Marta frowned, and Nikki went on. "Aunt Marta, trust me on this one. He thinks of you as a lot more than a friend. It's obvious. Didn't you see the expression on his face when the professor asked if he could show you the sights? *And*—" she spoke quickly over her aunt's indignant sigh "—speaking of the professor, I think he's more than a little interested himself. Wow, two guys at once. You think it could be that new perfume I gave you for Christmas?"

"I think you're impossible, that's what I think!" Marta said. "But I guess I'll keep you around, at least for laughs."

They drove onto the well-manicured grounds of the campus, and to Nikki's winter-weary eyes, the green of palms and madrone and the bright splashes of color from poppies and bougainvillea bordering the athletic fields were beautiful. On the way to the main part of the campus, the road followed the shoreline along the edge of high bluffs, through a wide, grassy area that extended toward the university buildings for at least 500 feet. On the perimeter of the area were tall eucalyptus trees with long strips of peeling bark curling down from the bare, gray-white trunks and ornate stone benches, which gave the area the appearance of a park.

Though the sky was beginning to darken, Nikki could still make out the waters of the Pacific far below. They were calm, reflecting the last orange glow of the sunset. She was taking in as much of the beauty as she could when Marta braked sharply, and the Grand Am came to an abrupt halt.

"Hey, what's up?" Nikki cried, startled.

The road turned away from the bluffs at that point and ran inland toward the buildings, and their progress was suddenly blocked by a crowd of people holding signs and placards. There must have been 50 or 60 people, Nikki estimated.

"What's all this about?" she asked.

"Looks like the end of a demonstration, I guess, but I can't tell what for." Marta's eyes narrowed as she strained to make out what was written on the signs. "Preserve the Islands for Our Children," she read slowly from one. As they watched, the crowd began to break up into small groups in front of the idling car. A uniformed policeman waved the groups to the side of the road so Marta and the two cars that had pulled up behind them could get through. "I'm not surprised—this campus is known as a kind of unofficial headquarters for environmentalists, animal rights activists, all that kind of stuff. Every time I've been here, they've had demonstrations of one kind or another."

They eased their way through the closely packed groups, and some of the demonstrators turned and stuck their signs up to the front window of the car and held them there until they nearly touched the glass. They leaned close to the side windows as the Grand Am passed through and yelled, *"Save the islands!"* and *"No more oil spills!"*

"Wow! Kind of an in-your-face attitude, isn't it?" Nikki said, amazed at their boldness.

Marta gave a short laugh. "This is nothing. One year, some demonstrators simply refused to move at all—I think because the television reporters were here that time—and traffic had to turn around and come in at the west entrance, about two miles from here."

Dr. Alexandra Fortenay, the sociology professor and codirector with Marta of the conference, was still in her office at the university. Nikki caught a quick glimpse of her through the narrow glass panel in the office door as Marta knocked.

The desk was heaped with work, and in the yellow circle of light from the green-shaded desk lamp, Alex's head was bent in concentration over one of the papers. Her glossy black hair was pulled back severely from her face, and when she glanced up at the sound of Marta's knock, Nikki could see that the hairstyle accentuated her high cheekbones.

"Come in!" Dr. Fortenay called, and all through her reunion with Marta, Nikki watched her, fascinated. When she pushed back the desk chair and stood up, she revealed her unusually tall and slender frame. *She's at least six feet,* Nikki thought. Nikki also noticed that all her words were accompanied by expansive gestures. *It's almost like she's on stage and knows she's playing to an audience.*

Marta turned and pulled her niece closer with a quick hug and introduced her. "Nicole, this is Alexandra Fortenay,

Dr. Alexandra Fortenay. She teaches sociology here."

"So you're Nikki," Dr. Fortenay said. She extended her long hands, palms up. Not sure what else to do, Nikki placed her own hands in them, and the cool, dry fingers closed over her own with a firm grip. "You should call me Alex. Everyone does. I'm delighted you could come along and enjoy our beautiful city. And help my daughter, MacKenzie. This is her spring break, of course, so I put her in charge of all the office details for the conference. But now she's gone and gotten herself involved in some research project with one of our biology professors, and it's taking far too much of her time."

Nikki, uncomfortable at having her hands held by this imposing woman, reclaimed them and moved back half a step.

"I was hoping MacKenzie might be around tonight," Marta said, "so Nikki could meet her."

Alex hesitated for a fraction of a second, then picked a speck of lint off the sleeve of her green silk pantsuit and dropped it into the wastebasket beside her desk before looking back up. "I, uh, I don't really think that will work out. Not tonight."

Alex and Marta shifted into an involved conversation about all the preparations they had to finish in the next four days before the conference began on Tuesday. When Alex mentioned the title of the paper she was to present—"Recursive Logic in the Gaian Cybernetic Cycle"—Nikki felt herself check out. She moved toward the window of Alex's office, which faced toward the ocean. A thin sliver of moon shone brightly near the horizon, reminding her of all the times she'd seen it shine that way over Lake Michigan.

She began thinking about all that had happened in the past year, and she was so deep in her memories that the click of the doorknob and the sound of the door opening startled her. She whirled around on one foot, just as Alex said, "MacKenzie!"

Nikki looked at the girl's sleek russet hair, cut in a wedge that fell from just a few inches long in back to midcheek in the front, and thought ruefully of the state her own hair was probably in. MacKenzie's full lips were adorned only with gloss, and she stood completely straight, yet at the same time relaxed, as though absolutely comfortable with every inch of her body.

Although she hadn't even moved, Nikki felt clumsy, awkward, and uneasy beside the older girl. *Good thing my mother isn't here,* she thought. She could just hear her mother's voice, *"You see, Nikki, why I'm always telling you to stand up straight?"*

"This is my daughter, MacKenzie," Alex said, and it was clear to Nikki that, while Alex's mouth formed a smile, her eyes were clouded, as though she was unhappy about something. "She's majoring in dance here, and she works at the university to help put herself through school."

A dancer, Nikki thought, looking at MacKenzie. *That explains why she looks so great.* Even in her simple black shorts and beige T-shirt that read EARTHKEEPERS in florid script across the front, she was elegant.

MacKenzie inclined her head slightly in one fluid motion to both Nikki and Marta and said a quiet "hello."

"Well, did you save the islands?" Alex asked, eyeing the placard that hung at her daughter's side, and Nikki realized suddenly that MacKenzie must have been one of the demonstrators.

"I guess we'll see, won't we?" MacKenzie answered curtly.

"MacKenzie's heavily into deep ecology. Or, I might say,

she's being influenced by a certain biology professor who's heavily into it."

"Let's talk about something else now, okay?" MacKenzie spoke to her mother as though to a slightly annoying child.

Nikki, embarrassed, turned so that she could study the pictures on the bookshelves behind Alex's desk.

"Well," Marta said, "we've gone over everything we need to for now, Alex. I think we'll find someplace to eat before we head for the hotel."

"Yes!" Nikki put in, glad to finally arrive at what seemed like a safe topic. "I've been starving ever since we got off the plane. I'd like a gigantic, juicy hamburger and some fries."

"I guess that settles where we're going then," Marta said. "Alex, would you and MacKenzie like to come with us?"

Alex shook her head no and gestured toward her paper-covered desk. But MacKenzie didn't even answer Marta's question. Instead, her eyes narrowed, and she looked intently at Nikki.

"You eat *meat?*"

There was so much disdain in her voice that Nikki felt the other girl might as well have said, "You have *leprosy?*" She wished, right down to her toes, that she'd never had a hamburger in her life, but it was a little late to be making that decision.

"Well, uh, yeah. I do," she stammered, then added a guilty, "sometimes." She'd been looking forward to meeting MacKenzie, to making a new friend here in California. *But,* she thought, *something tells me this isn't going to work out exactly like I'd planned.*

Four

WHEN NIKKI OPENED HER EYES the next morning, the hotel room was still and dark, and the glowing red numbers on the clock read 6:04. But she was wide awake and realized that in terms of her internal clock—which was set to eastern standard time—it was already past 9:00. *So,* she thought, *does this mean that I got to sleep in late or that I'm getting up really early?*

She slipped out of bed, pulled on heavy sweats, and made sure the electronic key card was stowed safely in her pocket before she left the room.

When the elevator doors slid open on the first floor, the rich aroma of coffee and donuts filled the air. In a sunken area of the lobby, round tables were set up next to a long table laden with coffee urns and an assortment of pastries and fruit. This time of the morning, the room was almost empty, except for a heavyset man leafing rapidly and noisily through the *Wall Street Journal,* the broad bald spot on top of his bent head shiny in the bright light of the lobby.

Then as Nikki made her way across the sunken area, she noticed someone else. He was a slender, dark-haired teenager not much taller than herself. He wore a faded denim jacket and moved so quietly that he seemed to appear out of nowhere. He quickly picked up two donuts and wrapped a napkin around them, then reached for an orange. As he did so, he scanned the room, and his nearly black eyes locked on Nikki's. His hand stopped in midair, and his elbows tightened against his sides.

Nikki looked away hurriedly and walked with forced nonchalance toward the glass doors leading to the pool and landscaped patio and the beach beyond, but even in that quick glance she couldn't help noticing his incredibly dark eyes, thickly fringed by long, black lashes.

As soon as the doors slid shut behind Nikki with a solid *click,* the sound of the ocean flowed over her. She watched, fascinated, as the dark water, which she could just make out in the dim gray of the foggy morning, ran in toward the shore. Over and over, at a point just a few hundred feet from the patio where she stood, the even surface of the ocean swelled, heaved higher and higher until gravity regained control, then crashed over on itself in a curling arc of white foam.

Nikki drew in a great breath of damp, fishy air and ran down the broad steps to the sand. It was growing lighter by the minute, light enough to place each foot safely as she jogged, and she started out faster than she should have, excited by the presence of the vast, thundering Pacific beside her and the firm, resilient sand beneath her feet.

She headed west to where the shore flung itself up into sharp, sudden cliffs that soon cut off the view of the hotel and town behind her. Nikki ran on and on, dodging boulders and twisted driftwood.

Nikki's breath grew more and more labored, and after a short 15 minutes, she slowed to a walk, arms dangling at her sides. The wide, sandy beach ended abruptly just ahead where one of the cliffs jutted out to the edge of the water. Hundreds of huge boulders were piled against its steep sides, but it was easy to see a pathway over the stones.

She clambered over the first boulder, then another. A few more minutes of careful climbing brought her to the top of the highest boulder. From there she scrambled onto the tablelike top of the cliff, where patches of wide, flat-blossomed beach flowers she couldn't name dotted the grass with pastel colors of yellow and pink.

She turned in a slow circle, drinking in the view. To the east, only shreds of fog remained in the sky, glowing faintly pink and purple as the sun came close to rising. The rest of the fog had settled itself out in the channel, blanketing the surface of the water like a huge quilted comforter. Above the puffy grayness, a purple line of pointed peaks marked the mountains of the channel islands. Nikki stared for a minute. Marta had mentioned the islands, but she'd had no idea they were so long or their mountains so massive.

Behind her, like a backdrop to the city, lay the mountains that sheltered Santa Linnea on the north. They were clear of fog, too, so that both behind and in front of her, mountains reared their heads into the sky—sharp, pointed ranges separated only by the flat strip of land where the city nestled beside the ocean.

Nikki needed a rest. She eased herself onto the sandy grass at the point of the cliff and stretched out her legs toward the edge, her back propped against one of the great boulders.

Once the noise of her labored breathing quieted, she could hear the gulls crying, at times swooping so low on their way to the water that she could detect the feathery rustle of their wings just above her head. As the curved orange rim of the sun edged into view, both the shreds of fog in the sky and the top of the fog bank over the channel suddenly glowed a fiery coral, fringed in gold. The sun rose higher, and Nikki felt the first whispers of its warmth against her face. Far out over the face of the water, a long, straight line of pelicans glided in a sober train, elegant in their silence, each bird mirroring in the smallest detail the movements of the bird in front of it.

They don't tell you this part on those "National Geographic" specials Grandpa loves so much, she thought. *They can't tell you how magical it all is when you're really here, with the waves crashing and the gulls crying all around and the ocean air blowing fresh across your face.*

She thought how she and Jeff Allen had sat side by side on the dune beside Lake Michigan the summer before. For as long as she could remember, Nikki had spent every summer at the Lake Michigan shore with her grandparents, and the Allens had come from their home in Chicago to their summer house next door.

There were six members of the Allen family—the parents; the 12-year-old twins; Carly, who was a year younger than Nikki; and Jeff, a year older. Carly, Jeff, and Nikki had been inseparable since they were toddlers, and Nikki missed them. Especially Jeff. How he would revel in the magnificent view before her now! She wished, fiercely for a moment, that he could see it with her, then reminded herself that that was another bad move she'd made this year—pushing Jeff away again and again until he'd decided that all he could ever safely be to her was a friend.

She watched until the birds were out of sight, then took a deep breath. *Okay. Time to think about something else here. God,* she said silently, *I promised myself that I would pray every day on this trip, especially for Evan. So here I am.* She paused for a moment, trying to fight down the doubts that always seemed to nibble at the edges of her thoughts when she prayed.

This is crazy, the doubts seemed to say, *sitting here talking to no one. What makes you think anybody's really listening? Maybe you just lost it that day you thought you became a Christian. You were pretty emotional, you know, giving Evan up for adoption and all—*

"Stop it!" she told herself sternly, then shifted her position on the scrubby grass and started again.

Lord, I told You I would pray for Evan every day, and that's what I'm trying to do right now. She thought of a conversation she'd had with her grandfather the week before. She'd sheepishly admitted her doubts to him, convinced she was the only one who had ever had such problems, and she was surprised when he acknowledged he'd gone through the same struggle. He had showed her a story in Mark chapter 9, and what the man in the Bible story prayed had become almost a daily prayer for Nikki.

Lord, I do believe. Help my unbelief. It always helped, at least a little, when she just acknowledged the struggles she was having. It was almost as though God didn't the mind the doubts as much as He did her trying to hide them. She was able to go on then, praying for her son, Evan, for the family that adopted him, and—

Nikki was concentrating so hard that the soft sound of

footsteps brushing through the dry grass startled her. She peeked around the side of the large boulder she was leaning against to see who was there. She held her breath as she watched. What had given her the idea it was safe to be out here alone before it was completely light?

As the figure came into view, she could see it was someone slight and dark-haired, walking quickly across the flat top of the bluff toward the far side, obviously unaware that she was there. As soon as she saw his denim jacket, Nikki recognized him as the boy who'd been helping himself to donuts and oranges at the hotel's continental breakfast.

The guy with the gorgeous eyes, she thought.

In just a moment, he had crossed over the bluff, then disappeared. Nikki stood up and followed curiously, wondering where he was going. She made sure she gave him enough time to get a good way ahead of her, then she jogged slowly in the same direction he'd gone.

She stopped abruptly at the edge of the bluff. Before her stretched a secluded, half-moon-shaped cove, shut in by the cliff on which she stood and another just like it that jutted out into the surf about a half mile up the beach. In between, high, steep banks crowned with eucalyptus trees stood like sentinels over the deserted stretch of sand.

Among the trees, a small building sat perched near the very edge of the bluff, and in front of it, leaning down the face of the cliff, was what looked like the remains of another building, boards and other materials dangling from it.

Nikki scanned the cove, trying to see where the boy had gone. Between the cliff where she stood and the next cliff was a huge crevice, perhaps 20 feet deep, spanned only by a narrow arch of sandstone. The waves, which for years had eaten the soft rock away beneath the arch, were already rushing into the cavern, over and over, as the tide came in.

There, at the far side of the arch, the boy was making his way carefully over the narrow path across its top. When the waves receded, Nikki could see how, at low tide, it would be possible to get to the bottom of the crevice by a jagged sort of path that ran diagonally down the bluff, then up the other side. But now, with the waves pounding in, the only way across was the bridge of stone.

Nikki watched the boy stop suddenly and steady himself when a huge wave surged into the crevice and sprayed water high into the air. The water forced under the stone bridge and into the narrow cavern on the other side had no place else to go but skyward. Even standing where she was, on a wide, flat piece of ground, Nikki felt dizzy looking down into the swiftly swirling water. She was amazed that anyone could keep his balance suspended on the sidewalk-thin arch over those waves.

When he finally started to move again, then reached the other side and disappeared once more from her view, Nikki let out a sigh of relief, surprised to find she'd been holding her breath until he got safely across.

There was something fascinating about the whole scene. She leaned farther over the edge to watch, then leaped back as another wave slammed into the opening and water shot high over her head.

Nikki watched it happen over and over again and thought how exciting it would be to stand in the middle of that stone arch if she could get up the nerve. She timed the waves mentally, calculating how long it would take to cross the bridge without getting wet. She inched her way toward it, then jumped back as another wave swept through the stone opening.

Nikki flexed her fingers, then clenched them into a fist and flexed them again as she watched. She waited until a wave crested and started to recede, then put one foot against the wet, dark rock of the bridge. She took another step but stopped as she heard the thunder of the next wave approaching. Then she made the mistake of looking down.

A wall of water swept into the cavern beneath her, crashing against its sides with a force that shook even the rock where she stood, and suddenly everything below her was in motion, first into the hollowed-out space of the cavern, then out, the water swirling and foaming, then sliding backward toward the sea, tumbling pebbles and shells and kelp in its grasp. Her eyes fixed on the roiling water beneath her feet, she struggled to maintain her balance.

Nikki turned and crept back the few inches she'd come, her heart pounding and her breath coming in gasps, and felt the spray soak the legs of her sweatpants.

She stood shivering as the breeze touched the heavy, wet material to the bare skin of her ankles and calves, then started back toward the hotel, running faster than she'd intended.

Five

IT WAS NOON WHEN NIKKI pulled the red Grand Am into the parking lot of the Beach Plum, where she'd agreed to meet Aunt Marta, Alex, and MacKenzie for lunch.

Aunt Marta was at the restaurant ahead of her and already had a table under one of the shining brass ceiling fans. Nikki made her way through the dining room crowded with rattan chairs and round, glass-topped tables, and greeted her aunt.

"Hello, Nik," Marta replied. "Alex and MacKenzie should arrive any minute." She handed a menu across the table to Nikki, who decided quickly on a hamburger and salad.

When she looked up, Marta was watching her closely, the skin between her eyebrows etched with the two vertical lines that always meant she was fretting over something.

"What?" Nikki asked. "What's the matter?"

"You're sure it's still okay with you—helping out at the office? I mean, it sounded like such a good idea when Alex and I talked about it on the phone. It meant you could be involved a little, meet some of the people at the conference.

But sometimes I forget, when I haven't been around Alex for a while, what an overwhelming person she can be."

Nikki looked at her aunt, who was wearing a beige-plaid jumper and white shirt, which still showed faint creases from the suitcase. *No one would ever call Aunt Marta particularly pretty,* she thought. *But once you get to know her, with her quick mind and crazy sense of humor and generous-to-a-fault heart, her looks don't matter.* Nikki smiled across the table at her.

"Hey, stop worrying," she said. "I'm fine with it. I think it'll be fun."

She was rewarded by the sight of the lines fading as Marta's face relaxed.

"Well, that's a relief. And it should only mean a couple afternoons, until we get everything up and running. Besides, this way you can get to know MacKenzie better."

At that, Nikki shrugged noncommittally and looked down at the menu again. She thought back to the hotel room, where she'd tried on five different outfits before settling on one. The whole time, she'd kept picturing MacKenzie, who could probably manage to look stunning in a flannel bathrobe, eyeing each outfit she tried with disdain.

"That's not exactly your idea of a fun afternoon, is it?" Marta added, and Nikki was amazed, as always, at how easily her aunt read her thoughts.

"I could think of a few other things I'd rather do," she admitted.

Marta's smile faded. "You know, Nikki, sometimes people who look the most in control are the most scared on the inside."

Nikki didn't answer because Alex and MacKenzie arrived just then, but her thoughts rolled on. *MacKenzie? Scared?*

You're usually right on target about people, Aunt Marta, but this time you missed it completely. Totally.

After they gave the waiter their orders, Nikki listened as Alex described the office tasks that would fall to her over the next few days.

"The biggest job is getting all the conferees' folders assembled. You'll be making endless copies of the papers that will be presented, collating them, then putting them into folders."

"Along with all the meal and seminar schedules and maps of the campus for people staying in dorms," MacKenzie added.

Soon, the waiter interrupted their conversation, efficiently balancing all four plates along the length of his arm. Nikki's burger and Marta's turkey club looked unsophisticated beside Alex's whole wheat pita that bulged with alfalfa sprouts and other vegetables and MacKenzie's tabouli. Nikki wished she had at least a clue what *tabouli* was.

As soon as the food was settled in front of them, Alex picked up the conversation again. She seemed to be able to talk and eat at the same time with no problem. MacKenzie, however, sat gracefully straight, now and then sipping sparkling water and forking up tiny bites of tabouli, her dark, almond-shaped eyes a little distant, as if she had more important things on her mind.

Nikki, who had been up for hours and had skipped breakfast, was ravenous. She was savoring her second generous mouthful of hamburger when she felt MacKenzie's eyes watching her. Nikki hesitated and the steaming meat dripped red-brown juice down her fingers and onto the plate beside the green slice of dill pickle.

MacKenzie gave a pointed sigh, then shrugged off her jacket. On her T-shirt, printed above the picture of a beautiful calf with large, long-lashed brown eyes, were the words I Don't Eat Anything That Has a Face.

Nikki studied the burger in her hands for a moment, then swallowed hard. She laid it back on her plate, picked up her fork, and started on her salad, trying to chew the crunchy red cabbage and crisp radishes quietly as she listened to Alex.

Alex quickly finished her pita sandwich, then leaned forward, her elbows on the table, her long fingers, weighted with heavy, ornate silver rings, cradling a glass of iced coffee. "Let me assure you though, Nikki, that it's not *all* work around here. I hear you have a trip to one of the islands planned for Saturday. We took Marta last year, and she loved it."

Marta nodded in agreement. "It was fantastic. Ted's going with us this time. Wait till you see the wildlife out there, Nikki."

"Well, Andaluca—that's the island you're going to, Nikki—was in the news last week, but it wasn't for the wildlife," Alex continued. "At least, not the kind you're talking about, Marta. It's so secluded out there that it's become the perfect point for smuggling drugs in from Mexico and South America."

"You're kidding!" Marta said.

"No. They bring in small planes late at night, flying without any lights, and drop weighted bales of drugs on the far side of the island at prearranged spots. Later on, divers go out and retrieve the bales. At first it was just marijuana, but now I understand there's heroin involved, too. The coast guard is overworked as it is around here, and there's no way they can constantly patrol the entire coastline. So the oil companies are saying that if they could use the island for some experimentation they want to do, they'd provide a round-the-clock presence that would keep drug dealers away. On the other hand, environmentalists say the oil companies are making up all these allegations about drugs just so—"

"And they're totally right," MacKenzie broke in. "Lee Tierney says the oil companies have been angling to use that island and the caves on it for years."

Alex looked back at MacKenzie, and her red lips closed in a thin, tight line before she went on. "In light of Tierney's long-running efforts to have marijuana and other drugs legalized, I'm not as sure as you are of his impartial stance on the issue."

Mother and daughter stared at each other for a few tense seconds. Nikki looked from one to the other and back, and she chewed her cabbage faster as she waited. Then the tension seemed to drain from Alex, and she went on as if nothing had happened.

"At any rate, the battle's been raging for months now." She touched the cloth napkin to her lips and pointedly changed the subject. "Marta, you and Nikki probably saw on the news just how devastating the winter rains were here this year."

Marta nodded, her mouth full of turkey, and Alex went on to describe the damage from the rains.

"The creeks filled up in just an hour or so, and when the tide came in and the full creeks tried to drain into the ocean, we had major flooding in the canyons. The beach areas were hit hard, too. We lost a couple gorgeous homes built too close to the cliffs. But anyway, enough about us. I want to hear all about you, Nikki. Otherwise—" she apologized with a little shrug of her shoulder "—I get talking and the time just disappears." She spread her hands wide, as though she didn't quite understand this phenomenon. "Marta tells me you are a pianist, like her. Tell me what you play."

Nikki hesitated, nervous under the gaze of those intense, heavy-lidded eyes. "Uh, well, to begin with, I'm *not* a pianist like Aunt Marta. I mean, she's really good and I'm . . . well, I'm nowhere near as good as she is."

"What music do you enjoy playing most?"

"I really like Debussy. And I like the Postimpressionists. And Bach."

Alex leaned forward even farther, her eyes bright. She went off into a long speech about some composer named Paul Winter and a full-scale choral mass he'd composed. She was soon wrapped up in her own words again, her elegant hands punctuating her sentences in the air as she spoke.

Nikki, smiling and nodding, found she was beginning to daydream, seeing in her mind the dark-haired boy making his way cautiously across the wet sandstone arch that morning. Then she realized that Alex's words had stopped abruptly in midsentence.

Nikki followed the older woman's gaze and found herself looking at Lee Tierney, who was threading his way between the tables right toward them. He wore a sports coat and jeans and appeared, if possible, even better-looking than he had on the plane the day before.

MacKenzie called out to him. "Lee! Hello!"

His easy, relaxed smile wrinkled his tanned nose. He leaned across the table and extended his hand to Alex, then cupped his hands briefly on MacKenzie's shoulders, and Nikki noted with surprise the faint blush creeping across MacKenzie's cheeks.

Lee smiled at Marta and asked if she was all settled in, but when he glanced at Nikki, he jerked backward suddenly in mock surprise, then looked pointedly at her glass of Coke. "Just checking," he said, relaxing his stance and grinning.

Now it was Nikki's turn to feel her cheeks flush hot and red, and she cringed in embarrassment, sure he would retell the whole story in front of MacKenzie and Alex. Instead, he caught her off guard. He stood there watching her for a second, tugging at his earlobe.

"You're looking great, Nikki. I've always been partial to long, dark hair on pretty girls."

Nikki glanced up at him in surprise, just in time to see MacKenzie's eyes narrow at her.

Well, that's two. One more strike and I'm out, I guess, Nikki thought. *Working with someone who can't stand the sight of me promises to be a real joy!*

MacKenzie, her face back to its usual impassive expression, spoke up. "Why don't you join us, Lee?"

Alex set her iced coffee on the table and slid back her chair. "Actually, I think we're nearly through," she said, "and I, for one, have a lot of work to get done this afternoon."

Lee Tierney regarded Alex evenly. "I'm meeting a friend for lunch anyway." He turned to MacKenzie. "But thank you, MacKenzie. I appreciate your kindness."

Nikki wondered if it was just her imagination working overtime, or if she'd really heard a slight emphasis on the word *your.* The biology professor had been polite enough, even charming, to each of them, but Nikki knew for sure that Alex was not impressed.

Six

THE PLACE WHERE NIKKI WAS TO WORK, a kind of communal workroom just outside MacKenzie's and several other cubbyhole offices, was lined on one side with floor-length windows overlooking an aquamarine cove. The tinted glass softened the harsh sunlight but did nothing to block her view of paragliders sailing off a cliff halfway down the cove and riding the air currents out over the ocean, suspended beneath brightly colored bands of lime-green, fuchsia, and yellow material that billowed above their heads. Farther out in the water, a crowd of surfers in black wetsuits lay stretched out on their boards, treading water, waiting for the next big wave.

Nikki watched in fascination as a huge swell gathered strength and rolled in toward the shore. The surfers scrambled madly, and at least a dozen managed to ride the wave toward the shore, their feet and knees working constantly to provide a graceful balance. One black-suited figure twirled around twice as he rode the crest of the wave, and Nikki's mouth dropped open.

"Wow!" she cried. "Look at that guy! Did you see him, Aunt Marta?"

When she whirled around to get Marta's attention, she came face-to-face with MacKenzie and was suddenly aware that her voice must have been much louder than she intended.

MacKenzie's eyebrows lifted almost imperceptibly, but all she said was, "I'll show you around as soon as you're ready, Nikki."

After Marta left for her afternoon committee meeting, Nikki trailed MacKenzie from table to table, listening to instructions on how to run the copy machine, which papers needed to be copied first, and where to find the extra reams of paper in the storage closet. She tried hard to keep her eyes off the wall of windows and the paragliders and surfers outside.

She made several attempts to start a casual conversation, but making small talk with MacKenzie was a lot like trying to push a lawn mower through waist-high grass. It just kept bogging down. To Nikki's query about how long she had lived in Southern California, MacKenzie said simply, "All my life." When Nikki asked what kind of dance she liked best, MacKenzie answered, "All kinds."

The only time she showed any flicker of interest was when she was helping Nikki reload the copy machine with staples for the last 50 copies of Alex's paper, "Recursive Logic in the Gaian Cybernetic Cycle," and Nikki commented, "Your mother is incredibly intelligent."

MacKenzie positioned the staples in the holder, then glanced at Nikki. "She certainly thinks so."

Nikki looked up, surprised. "Why do you say that?"

MacKenzie rolled her eyes. "Just listen to her. At the drop

of a hat, she launches into all her outmoded theories about religion and social interaction and—"

"Outmoded?" Nikki interrupted. "What do you mean?"

MacKenzie clicked the staple compartment shut and reset the printer controls. "Our first priority these days has to be taking care of the world around us. If we solve our environmental and ecological problems, human behavior will take care of itself. Dr. Tierney says ecology is absolutely the only solution."

Nikki looked at her, puzzled. "Wait a minute. How is solving environmental problems supposed to fix human behavior? I mean, people do stuff that's wrong, no matter what their environment is like."

MacKenzie sighed. "Wrong, right—those concepts are so outdated, Nikki. There was a time when people believed that because it was all they could understand. Now we know that behavior is basically a matter of being enlightened."

Nikki took fresh copies, each of them 12 pages, from the collating trays. She inserted them one by one into maroon folders, then stacked them on top of the high pile that already sat on the long, wood-grained table. She was pretty sure that what MacKenzie was saying was wrong, but she couldn't figure out what to say in return.

"Anyway, if you start talking in terms of *right* and *wrong*," MacKenzie continued, "then you have to believe in some mythical being—some god—who has authority to say what's right and what isn't. I prefer to trust what I can see, not some invisible person who's supposed to know everything."

Nikki opened her mouth, but MacKenzie was on a roll. "Because that's practically from the Dark Ages, you know? I mean, it's the basis for a very crude way of relating to other humans. Everyone knows that religious intolerance is responsible for nearly all the wars in the world. And now we know that what people have always called *God* is just the life force that connects us all. It's nothing more or less than the power of our collective mind. So we ought to be concentrating on our responsibility to our home, the earth." She checked the paper tray. "While I'm here, I may as well load more paper for you. It's getting low."

Nikki slid more copies out of the trays and balanced them on top of the others, thinking about all that had happened to her in this past year, wondering if her behavior would have changed if she'd been *enlightened*, whatever that meant. She remembered how Jeff Allen had struggled to explain Christianity to her, even when it was awkward for him, and imagined where she would be now if he hadn't.

Nikki looked at MacKenzie's flawless skin and watched her load the paper with quick, graceful movements. MacKenzie was so confident, so sure her convictions were right. Nikki felt a small stir of envy, wishing her own beliefs were that solid. Instead, the words she'd just heard created a kind of burning inside her. What if God—the God she'd trusted to save her just a few weeks ago—wasn't any more than what MacKenzie had said? What if He really wasn't there at all? That couldn't be right, could it? What about Jesus dying and coming back to life?

Nikki burst out, "If you don't think anything is right or wrong, MacKenzie, then how do you explain feeling guilty about something you've done?"

"Feeling *guilty?*" The taller girl gave an exaggerated sigh. "Wait, don't tell me. You grew up in the Bible Belt, right? Next you'll be telling me you're some kind of religious fundamentalist." She gave a short laugh and looked at Nikki as though they were sharing a joke, as though no one in her right mind would ever admit to that. "Guilt is nothing more than a conditioned response to an archaic thought system like . . . like Christianity. Or Judaism." She checked the copier controls again. "There. You should be all set now. I'm going back to my office to finish recording some test results Lee wants. Let me know if you have any problems, okay?"

Great, Nikki thought, trying hard to come up with something intelligent to say before MacKenzie got out of earshot. *Everything I just started believing is now an "archaic thought system."*

She added the last few folders to the pile and started to speak, but she never got to say a thing. Those last few folders proved to be too much and half the stack shifted suddenly, then toppled. Nikki grabbed at them and ended up knocking the other half of the stack to the floor.

MacKenzie turned and looked down at the mess, then back at Nikki. She sighed and said, "I'll be in my office."

Nikki watched her disappear inside and shut the door firmly behind her.

"Nice work," Nikki muttered under her breath. "And for your second act, maybe you can make an absolute fool of yourself again *tomorrow.*" She sighed and crouched to the floor, gathering up armfuls of the maroon folders.

Why couldn't she think of anything to say back to MacKenzie when she'd needed to? Maybe she wasn't really a Christian at all. Maybe it didn't . . . *take* . . . somehow, when she'd prayed that day.

Nikki stared at the stack of folders in her arms. In the light of MacKenzie's scornful attitude, it seemed highly unlikely that anything had really happened inside her that day, except for her emotions running wild.

Who was she, anyway, to think God would forgive *her?* Especially after how she'd messed up. Nikki struggled to get to her feet, trying to ignore the sinking feeling in her stomach.

Early that evening, Nikki nursed her crumbled pride while lying on a cushioned chaise lounge beside the hotel pool, soaking up the last of the day's sunshine. Every muscle was relaxing and unwinding, and she probably would have dozed off if she hadn't kept opening one eye and checking periodically to see if the boy with the denim jacket would turn up.

She let her thoughts drift to MacKenzie, about how things between them had certainly gotten off on the wrong foot. She thought about the Allens, back in Illinois, too. The weatherman on the evening news had made a big deal about a spring snowstorm that was sweeping through Chicago, which meant Gram and Grandpa on the eastern shore of Lake Michigan would probably get hit with snow in a few hours. With her eyes shut tight, she tried to envision snow falling but failed. The feel of sunshine and the sound of birds chirping made it almost impossible to remember what a snowstorm felt like.

Nikki grinned, remembering Carly Allen's response when she found out Nikki was coming to Santa Linnea with Aunt Marta. "I can just see it now—sunshine, flowers, beaches! And I have to stay here in *this* weather! Aaaggghhh! I can't stand it!"

Carly had suggested they keep in touch through E-mail while Nikki was gone. "The least you can do is give us a blow-by-blow description of what it's like out there," she'd said, "since you're the only one lucky enough to get to go!"

Nikki felt a shiver run down the length of her body and opened both eyes. The sun had gone behind the hotel building, and the air was cooling rapidly. She checked around the pool once more, but there was no sign of the dark-eyed boy.

Back in the hotel room, Marta finished putting the last touches on her paper for the conference, then signed on to AOL and checked for messages.

"You have mail, kiddo," she told Nikki, who was standing in the bathroom doorway, brushing out her freshly shampooed hair.

"Oh, yeah? Must be from Carly. She wanted to keep in touch." *And maybe, just maybe, there'll be something from Jeff.* She pushed the thought away quickly.

"Not from Jeff?" Marta asked.

Nikki looked at her in mock surprise. "Aunt Marta, that's the closest I've ever heard you come to fishing for information!"

Marta grinned, then shrugged her shoulders and looked a little abashed. "You're right. I just didn't want to butt in. *But* since my attempts at tact are so woefully inept, I guess I'll just come right out and pry shamelessly. How are things going with Jeff these days?"

Nikki used the hairbrush in her hand to emphasize her words. "I have an even better idea. What do you say we make a deal? I'll tell you about Jeff, and you can tell me more about Ted. Wilcox, you know," she added, as Marta's eyes widened, "the one who's so interested in when you can make time to go out on that sailboat with him."

Marta looked at her steadily, one eyebrow raised. "Nikki, I think you've had too much sun. After that long, gray winter back home, this is probably a shock to your system, which would account for your losing your mind this way." She got up from in front of the computer, took her robe off a hanger, and disappeared into the bathroom, stopping just before she closed the door to say, "I know this will be a big disappointment to you—" there was a pause as she yawned loudly "— but I'm much too tired to get into the whole romance thing tonight."

The door clicked shut, punctuating her sentence. Then it opened again, just a crack. "And just for your information, there is *nothing* between Ted and me except 15 years of being good friends." There was another click, a firm one, but Nikki could hear in her aunt's voice that she was laughing.

"Yeah, sure. I can tell," Nikki called, her voice loud enough to carry through the closed door.

She heard both the fan and the shower go on in answer on the other side of the bathroom door and gave up. Nikki sat down at the desk and clicked on her mail, surprised to find that Jeff *had* written.

Hi, Nik,

Are you bored yet? Ha! Must be really tough out there with all that sun and the beach and everything. We're supposed to get five inches of snow tonight. Carly says hi—in fact, she's threatening me with instant death if I don't get up and let her type, but so far she's losing. We won our game with Grant City last night, which means we're in the finals. Pretty good, huh? I—

Hey, Nik! This is Carly. Jeff says to tell you he'll write more when I let him back on-line. (Which may be never!) So tell me all about it. What's it like out there? Have you been *to the beach yet? You'll probably have a killer tan and look absolutely gorgeous by the time you get back (and I'll still be white as a ghost) and all the guys in Michigan will fall all over themselves just to talk to you.*

Speaking of guys—have you met any? What are they like out there? You really need to let me know this stuff so I can give you advice (just kidding!). Listen, I've gotta go, but next time I'll tell you about the incredible guy who just moved in next door to us. Jeff says he'll never even look at a sophomore like me (he's one of the great exalted seniors, like Jeff!). Anyway, stay tuned—more later.

Love ya! Carly

Nikki laughed as she finished the message. It was almost like having Carly there with her, her blonde hair shining and her laughter filling the room. She clicked on *Reply* and started to type.

❦ *Seven* ❦

NIKKI WAS UP EARLY AGAIN the second morning, feeling the pull of the ocean stronger than ever. Her walk through the lobby was almost an exact replay of the previous morning. Even the man with the *Wall Street Journal* was in place again, one foot propped over his other knee in the exact same position. But this time she was actively looking for the boy in the denim jacket.

This time, he stood near the sliding doors in the shadow of one of the potted palms. Nikki was passing just behind another of the palms when he cast a tense, hurried glance around the room, and she knew he hadn't seen her. She hesitated there in the shadow.

This is almost like spying, she thought. *I should let him know I'm here.* Then she laughed at herself. *Don't be silly. This is a public place, and whatever he's doing is his own business.*

In the seconds that she hesitated, the boy moved silently to the buffet table, picked up a banana and an orange, and slipped them into the pockets of his jacket. His eyes scanned the room again, then he quickly tucked a bagel and some little jelly packets into a napkin and stuffed them into his pockets alongside the fruit.

Why on earth is he sneaking food? It seemed important to her to get away before he saw her, before he caught her watching him. She frowned and slipped silently to the door while his back was turned, the rubber soles of her shoes noiseless on the carpet.

The sun was rising by the time Nikki worked her way across the loose, dry sand to the waterline and started her run. There was no fog this morning, and the islands stood out of the channel in a stark, purple line, their peaks lit golden-red with the glow of the rising sun.

At the sandstone bridge, she stood a long time, watching the waves wash in and splash up out of the cavern. She was so deep in thought that the hollow *thunk* of a pebble falling against the boulders took a second to register, jarring her back to the present.

The boy from the hotel was crossing the bluff toward her, his jeans jacket thrown over one shoulder. A wave of fear swept over her but subsided at the look in his black eyes when he saw her. He was as startled as she felt. His coal-black hair, straight and shiny, had fallen down over his forehead and into his eyes. He tossed his head so that it fell back into place, then gave her a hesitant half nod.

"Hello." His voice held more than the trace of an accent, and the word trailed upward at the end so that it was more question than statement.

Nikki wondered briefly if she should try out her high school Spanish on him, but decided she'd rather not look that foolish.

"Hi," she answered. They stared at each other for another

moment, then Nikki said the obvious thing, the first thought that came to mind. "It's beautiful here, isn't it?"

The boy nodded, looking beyond her to the ocean. "Yes."

He seemed to struggle with himself for a minute, then he laid his jacket carefully on a large rock and came toward her. Though he looked about her age, he was no taller than she was, so that she was looking directly into his eyes. Nikki had the impression that he was working hard at acting nonchalant.

She wondered what would happen if she spoke her thoughts. *I know what's in your coat—I saw you stuffing all that food in your pockets.* But of course that wasn't the kind of thing she could come right out and say.

He continued, his speech oddly formal, as though he had to work to think of the right words. "You are from—around here?"

"No. From Michigan." In light of his accent, she went on. "It's back in the Midwest, near the Great Lakes."

"I know," he said simply, as though accustomed to people assuming he wouldn't know things. "This is your vacation?"

"Kind of," she answered. "I'm here with my aunt. She's part of a conference at the university."

They had moved, as they talked, away from the arch where the waves roared noisily, and toward the front of the bluff that looked down over a narrow strip of beach. Nikki's attention was caught by the movement of tiny white-and-gray birds no bigger than her hand on the sand far below, birds that seemed to be doing a curious dance with the water. Over and over, in the short interval between waves, the birds probed the sand with sharp jabs of their black, shiny beaks and then scurried back toward the cliffs, their sticklike legs pumping stiffly.

"Sanderlings," the boy said, nodding at them.

"Sanderlings?"

"Yes. They're a kind of sandpiper," he answered.

Nikki glanced sideways at him, surprised to see the intense interest in his long-lashed eyes, then quickly back at the beach. "What kind of bird is that? The black one there with the long, skinny neck that keeps diving into the water?"

He squinted, following the direction of her pointing finger. "That is called a cormorant. They dive very deep—" his short-fingered, square hands stretched far apart to illustrate his words "—and sometimes they even take bait off the fishermen's lines."

"You're kidding," Nikki said.

"No." He smiled at her surprise. "They can dive 70, 80 feet. Some die because they take not just the bait, but the hook as well. It gets caught inside them and. . . ." He finished the sentence with a shrug.

Nikki tried to picture a bird diving that far beneath the surface of the water, then continued. "I saw dolphins. Yesterday morning," she told him, and he nodded and smiled a little.

"I used to watch for dolphins, just at sunrise," he said. "Some people believe the whole day will be lucky if you see dolphins in the morning." He narrowed his eyes toward the water again as though he had given up expecting to see the curving, silvery backs break the surface. "I have not seen them in many days now." Then he looked back toward her. "What do you do while your aunt is at the university?"

"I'm helping out in the conference office a little. Other than that, I'm on vacation. I guess I'll just lie around in the sun. We don't see too much sunshine this time of year in Michigan, at least not hot sun you can lie out in. And I'll probably go see some tourist things, too. I hear there's a wharf with some little shops and stuff."

As she talked, Nikki was trying to think of a polite way to ask who he was, but he saved her that trouble.

"Your name is—?"

"Nikki. Nicole, actually—Nicole Sheridan, but nearly everybody calls me Nikki. How about you?"

He shot a quick glance at her eyes, and he seemed to be measuring her. "Antonio."

"Are you on vacation, too?"

The bones of his shoulders tightened under his gray T-shirt. "No."

Nikki sensed at once that she was trespassing on his privacy, but the next words were out of her mouth before she could stop them. "But I saw you at the hotel—the South Coast Inn." Then she kept the words coming quickly, trying to cover the panic she saw flash through his eyes as he darted a glance back at his jacket where it lay on the rocks. "That's where we're staying, my aunt and I. So I thought maybe you . . ."

Her voice died away, and after a long pause, Antonio answered stiffly, watching the toe of his sneaker as he kicked at the sand, "I . . . help out there. With maintenance."

"Oh." *That explains it then,* she thought, laughing inwardly at her cloak-and-dagger imagination. *If he works there, of course they'd let him eat there.* "Where do you live?"

He pointed inland with a backward jerk of his head. "Back there, by the airport."

Nikki thought of the cluster of run-down houses that she and Marta had seen when they pulled out of the airport parking lot the night they arrived. She wondered uneasily if those were the houses Antonio meant.

"Well," she said, trying to turn the conversation back to safer ground, "I was just going to walk farther down this way." She motioned toward the rock bridge and the cliffs beyond it.

"No!" The word seemed to burst out of him, then he struggled for control and spoke in his normal voice. "I mean, it is very dangerous to go that way. You see how narrow the bridge is?"

"Sure." Nikki laughed. "I got soaked trying to cross it yesterday."

Antonio shook his head emphatically. "You must not go there—the rock is very dangerous when it's wet. And beyond that, there are only more cliffs. The storms did much damage there. The cliffs could cave in any time. No one ever goes there anymore." He began urging her back toward the hotel. "Come this way and walk on the beach instead. It is much safer."

Antonio led her back down the sandy path and over the boulders. He didn't stop until he got Nikki off the cliff and turned back toward the hotel.

She bent over and pulled off her running shoes and socks, carrying them in her hands as she walked into the edge of a wave. "Whoa! This water's like ice!" she said, dancing backward, and Antonio nodded in agreement and gave his funny half smile again. "At least the sand's warming up from the sun," she added.

When the foaming water of the wave receded, Nikki leaned over to pick up a shell it had deposited on the beach. She fingered the knobby, glistening surface of the shell and traced the spiral pattern from its tip to its fluted, pinkish-brown edge. She turned the shell over and over, and the mother-of-pearl coating on the bottom flashed in the brilliant morning sunlight. Antonio stuck his hands into the pockets of his jeans and strolled along beside her.

"This is so pretty," she said, brushing the gritty wet grains of sand off it and holding it up once again to admire it.

Antonio smiled at her enthusiasm, a whole smile this time, as though he thought she was making far too much of an ordinary shell. "It is just a whelk. There are many of them."

"It's still pretty," Nikki insisted. She shook it gently to force the last drops of murky water from inside, then stuck the shell in the pocket of her shorts.

She reached down and picked up a small, gray rock with what appeared to be a miniature forest of pink plants growing from its surface. "What's this?"

Antonio reached out and took it from her hand, turning it over and over. "It is called a coralline." He rolled the *r* in the word effortlessly, and Nikki stared at him curiously, wishing she could do half as well in Spanish class.

Antonio averted his eyes quickly, then began talking about the coralline, explaining how algae attached to the rock and grew there. She noticed that this time he was careful *not* to roll the *r*, and she realized he was embarrassed.

"Where'd you learn all this stuff—about the birds and the shells and all?" she asked.

"At the university. A biology professor there has a room filled with tanks. They have all kinds of sea life in them, and sometimes I help him clean them out, and he tells me things." He stared at the waves and the islands beyond, then added so quietly Nikki could barely hear, "My mother taught me much, also."

Nikki went on searching the sand as they neared the hotel and felt the sun growing hotter against her bare arms. From the corner of her eye, she could see that Antonio kept glancing back over his shoulder toward the bluffs where he had laid his jacket. She had nearly made up her mind to ask him about it when she caught sight of what looked like a shining, transparent green shell, smooth and curved and shaped like no other she'd seen.

"Antonio!" she cried. "Look at this one!" She rubbed its silky wet smoothness between her fingers, then looked more closely. "What is it?"

Antonio struggled to keep his mouth straight, but she could hear the laughter behind his words. "I would say you have there a genuine piece of old Coke bottle." He shrugged. "Maybe Pepsi."

"You mean this is *junk?*" Nikki said. "But it's beautiful. And the edges are all smooth and—"

"Things left in the ocean a long time are always smooth. The water wears them down," he said. Then he turned and looked back down the beach. "I think I forgot my jacket on the cliff. I must go back."

Nikki looked straight into his black eyes for just a second. *He didn't forget at all, and he knows that I know it,* she thought. But she could see he was not going to offer any further explanation.

"Well, maybe I'll see you around the hotel," she said as she started up the stairs to the hotel patio.

Antonio smiled his uneasy half smile again and nodded, then turned and walked quickly down the beach the way they had come. Nikki watched him go, his back straight and taut as if he felt her eyes on him, and realized she'd just been escorted safely back to the hotel.

No, she corrected herself. *That's not exactly right. It's more like I was escorted away from something, something he didn't want me to see.*

❦ *Eight* ❧

SUNRISE WAS STILL HALF AN HOUR AWAY when Marta steered the Grand Am the length of the Santa Linnea wharf where they were to meet Ted. She eased it into a parking space, the car tires thudding loudly over the worn wooden timbers and turned cross timbers and turned off the engine.

"Don't forget to lock your door, Nikki."

Fog still shrouded Andaluca, one of the islands Nikki saw far out in the channel each morning when she ran, and she wondered how it would look close up when they finally docked there in a few hours.

Nikki climbed out of the car onto timbers dark with creosote. Long breakers rolled in underneath the wharf, crashing against the wooden pylons with a jolt that made Nikki look down nervously at the dark-green strands of kelp floating on the waves. Beside the wharf, the *Suncatcher* rocked gently back and forth in the water. Against a backdrop of gray sky and waves, three crew members in bright-orange waterproof jackets stood huddled next to the wooden wharf railings, their red hands curled around steaming Styrofoam cups.

"Coffee! That smells marvelous," Marta said, hugging her arms against her sides and shivering. "Is it for passengers, too, I hope? Or just for the crew?"

Ted walked up to join them as she spoke, shaking his head at her words. "Still hooked on caffeine, huh?"

Marta swung around at the sound of his voice and smiled. "I am, with absolutely no apologies. And good morning to you, too."

Ted and Marta accepted coffee from the crew with thanks, and even Nikki took a cup, more to warm her freezing fingers than to drink.

"See what I meant, Nikki?" Marta asked in between sips. "When I told you to wear everything you brought that's warm?"

Nikki nodded. "Yeah. I just don't think I brought enough, that's all. I never expected mornings to be so cold in California." She held her face close to the cup and let the hot steam warm her cheeks.

Other passengers had gathered around them now, waiting to board, and a heavyset woman bundled into several layers of shirts and jackets—Nikki could count four collars, at least—rubbed her hands together rapidly with a dry, papery sound. "Just wait till the sun comes up," she said. "We'll be shedding all this stuff faster than you can believe."

As they finally began to board, Nikki noted a panel truck with Channel 11 News emblazoned on the side pulling in beside the other passengers' cars. As two men unloaded a video case and other equipment from the truck, three more cars rattled over the bumpy wharf and found parking places. Doors flew open and passengers, who all looked about college age, made a dash for the small wooden building at the edge of the wharf that served as the *Suncatcher* ticket office.

Ted watched the commotion intently, then muttered, more to himself than to Marta and Nikki, "Looks like this tour's popular for more than just sightseeing."

Nikki was about to ask him what he meant when the line ahead of her moved and they were urged on by the people behind them.

By the time the *Suncatcher* pulled away from the dock, the throb of its motors vibrating the metal deck beneath her feet, the sun had risen completely. Its warmth against her face grew by the minute. Nikki slipped her white sweatshirt off first, then the sweatpants she'd pulled on over shorts. All around her, others were doing the same, laughing as they tried to fold articles of clothing tightly enough to fit into picnic baskets and backpacks.

"This is wonderful, Aunt Marta," Nikki said from her place by the railing. She surveyed the water and mountains and crystal-clear sky all around her. "It's like . . . like Michigan never even happened, like we're on some whole other planet. I can't even remember how things look all covered with snow, can you?" She closed her eyes, trying to picture the scene, but gave up.

"Well, I wouldn't go *that* far." Marta grinned. "I've put in about twice as many winters as you, so let's just say my memory's a little clearer."

Ted drained the last of his coffee, leaned over the rail, and crumpled the cup between his hands. "I've been telling her for years to move out here, Nikki. I told her she could completely forget about snow if she did, but so far I haven't made much progress."

Marta, who seemed glad for a legitimate chance to change the subject, spoke up. "Nik, look. See those people down on the other end of the deck? The ones who ran to get on at the last minute? Isn't that MacKenzie with them?"

Nikki looked in the direction her aunt pointed and saw a tall girl in the middle of the group of students, her russet-brown hair shining in the morning sun, her head visible above most of those around her. "Yeah, I guess it is," she said, trying to sound unconcerned. But inwardly, a voice was growling in her mind, *And here I thought today could just be fun.*

Then, so close behind Nikki that she jumped at the sound of it, a crew member's voice cried, "Dolphins!" and everyone crowded to their side of the boat to see. Nikki held her breath, staring hard at the water to distinguish any movement. Suddenly, a dark, pointed fin sliced the surface, followed immediately by another just a little behind and to the right, then both of them curved back into the water.

"Two! There're two of them!" voices cried, but the crew member shook his head and kept pointing.

"There are more than that," he said. "Keep watching. You have to learn to spot 'em."

"Three. No, *four!*"

People were counting excitedly, but from where Nikki stood, she could see even more of the pointed fins. In the end, they counted nine dolphins swimming beside the boat, their silvery backs flashing again and again, just above the surface of the water.

Some passengers hung over the edge of the boat, their hands stretched out, trying to get closer to the graceful swimmers in the water; others snapped picture after picture, trying to synchronize their camera shutters with the brief instants that backs protruded from the water. The cameraman from Channel 11 was shooting as much footage of the excited passengers as of the dolphins. Nikki leaned over the metal rail with the others, stretching her arm toward the point where she'd seen the dolphins. She couldn't help remembering Antonio's words: *"Some people believe the whole day will be lucky if you see dolphins in the morning."*

It was well over an hour before the *Suncatcher* brought them close enough to the islands that Nikki could start distinguishing the live oaks and huge masses of bright yellow that Ted called coreopsis—"a kind of sunflower that grows on big bushes like trees"—coloring the smooth, green hillsides.

Rugged cliffs towered straight up from the beach on either side of the meadows, and Marta pointed out two waterfalls that spilled over the jagged cliff faces into the surf far below. As the boat rounded one of the cliffs, a cave came into view, a cave so huge the ship could easily have sailed inside.

"There are caves all along these islands," Ted commented when Nikki pointed it out. "When the tide is out, you can walk right into the back of this big one here. And there are ledges you can climb up on that lead even farther back into the cave."

In the glare of bright sunlight that sparkled on the water, it was impossible to see the back wall and judge how deep it might actually be.

"What happens when the tide comes in?" Nikki shivered, staring at the dark mouth of the cave and thinking how the tide slammed into the cavern where she jogged in the mornings.

"Oh, I don't think you'd get trapped or anything," Ted answered. "You might get cold and bored, but there'd be plenty of places where you could stay up out of the water."

They watched as the captain maneuvered the boat smoothly toward the tiny island dock. The small length of beach around it looked to Nikki like it was littered with large, gray boulders, but as she watched, one of them moved. Marta laughed at her surprised expression.

"This is Diablo Cove, and it's known for these elephant seals that breed here. They're the biggest seals around."

"Those are *animals?*" Nikki asked. "Until I saw that one move, I thought this was just a really rocky beach."

"They're pretty quiet right now. Wait till one of them decides to flop his way down to the water," Marta said. "The males are so huge, you can't imagine how they could ever get all that bulk moving."

"They can weigh a couple thousand pounds," Ted put in, "so it's a pretty impressive sight."

Nikki watched closely, hoping to see another of the seals move, but there was only the occasional flicker up and down of a sand-covered flipper. As the boat docked, her inspection of the seals was interrupted by the noise of people coming her way. Nikki turned around and found herself face-to-face with MacKenzie and the group of students.

They were talking intently on their way up the ramp to the dock. MacKenzie was the only one who even noticed Nikki, Marta, and Ted standing there. Surprise crossed her face, then she nodded and said a cool "hello" as she passed.

Nikki had just enough time to note MacKenzie's T-shirt of the day. The silk-screen picture on the front was a large, blue sphere showing North and South America, with hints of other continents around the perimeter. Across the top, following the curve of the globe, the words in magenta script read, LOVE YOUR MOTHER.

Ted and Marta were in no hurry, so MacKenzie's group had disappeared in another direction by the time they and Nikki made their way down the gangplank, then even farther down the pier steps to the thin crescent of beach.

Nikki walked closer to the seals, trying hard to see the trunklike snouts that Ted said gave the elephant seal its name, but most of the animals had their heads turned away from her.

"You better not go too close, Nikki," Ted warned.

The seals looked as though they hadn't moved in days and had no intention of doing so now.

"I'm okay!" she called back. "I think they're all asleep."

Then suddenly, the quiet broke. One huge seal behind Nikki reared its long-trunked head upward with a hoarse, snorting bellow. It began moving directly toward her in an awkward, shambling motion that belied how quickly it was actually covering the sand. Nikki shrieked and started moving backward, only to stumble and nearly fall over a smaller seal half hidden in the sand beside her. She turned and ran as fast as she could back to where Ted and Marta were standing, her heart pounding.

Marta let out a sigh of relief and opened her mouth to speak.

"Don't say it!" Nikki said first, both her hands up to ward off her aunt's comments. "I learned my lesson. And believe me, with a thousand pounds of blubber coming right at you, it's *easy* to learn!"

Ted was laughing hard, bent nearly double. "Oh, man, Nikki—if you could have seen the look on your face when he first came after you!" He broke off, trying to get hold of himself.

The three of them stood watching as the seal continued its trek to the water. It traveled only about 20 feet, then sprawled flat in the sand again for long minutes, apparently exhausted.

Eventually, the seal started up again, moving another 10 feet or so before stopping to rest. In that way, in fits and starts, the animal finally made it to the surf, where he slid into the water and disappeared from view. By that time, several other seals were following his lead.

"Looks like we're disturbing them," Ted said. "Let's go hike the trails, then I'll show you the cave when we come back. We'll have to wait for the tide to go out a little more anyway until we can go inside." He looked sideways at Nikki. "How about if you stay close, Nikki? I don't think I want you risking any more close encounters with the wildlife."

❦ *Nine* ❦

THEY SPENT THE NEXT FEW hours climbing what seemed like endless steps to the meadows and exploring the wilderness there and on top of the cliffs. Nikki stood at the edge of one of the streams, watching as it ran out of land and plunged over the side of a cliff in a delicate waterfall, and she breathed in big breaths of the mixture of sea- and flower-scented air.

"Mmmm, what's that smell? Kind of sweet and spicy at the same time?" Nikki asked.

Ted tore off a small, spiny piece from a gray-green shrub and held it out for Nikki to sniff.

"Sage. It grows all over the place out here." He turned to Marta and gestured at the open meadow in which they were standing. "Ready for a rest?" he asked, and she nodded.

He pulled a well-worn blanket from his backpack, spread it on the grass, and motioned for them to sit down. He explained some of the history of the islands as they sat, Marta hugging her knees to her chest and staring back over the 20-mile-wide channel to the mainland, which was clearly visible from there. Nikki stretched out on her stomach as she listened, her sneaker-clad feet in the air, and pulled the sprig of sage to pieces, bit by bit, each torn spot releasing more of the pungent odor.

"The Chumash Indians lived here a long time ago, then settlers took over," Ted said. "Some became ranchers and raised livestock here, but now the land belongs to the government and is one great wildlife preserve."

"Can you imagine," Marta said dreamily, "this whole island being your own ranch? With the ocean all around you, and a big house up here on top of this hill?"

"One with lots of huge windows so you could see out in every direction?" Ted questioned softly.

Marta nodded.

"That's quite a picture," he said.

Nikki had the feeling that they'd completely forgotten she was even there. She rolled over and sat upright. "Do you bring your boat out this far, Ted?"

"Only when I know I can trust the weather. Getting caught out here when the weather's iffy—that's not my idea of fun."

Marta stretched her legs out in front of her on the blanket and worked her feet back and forth and side to side as though they were stiff. "Besides," she said, "Ted's always got too many extracurricular projects going to do much pleasure sailing. Tell Nik about the party your church is having tonight."

Ted grinned. "It's the end of a little project we got involved in, an *extracurricular* project, as your aunt would say. We've been sponsoring a Vietnamese family that immigrated, and they've done very well. They bought a little restaurant down in Thousand Oaks, and they're moving there in a few days. So we're having a farewell party for them tonight."

Nikki crushed the last of the sage sprig between her fingers and sniffed the scent. "What do you mean, you sponsored a family?"

"Oh, we find housing and jobs for them—usually with people in our own church if that's at all possible—and try to help with clothes and food, toys for the kids, stuff like that. People usually need help with all the government red tape and with learning English, too. Our church just tries to give them plenty of attention and friendship. It's not easy, leaving everything you're used to and starting over again in a strange country."

"Sounds like a lot of work for you," Nikki said.

"I suppose," Ted answered and leaned back on his elbows. "But we started this project about five years ago when I was preaching through the book of James, and we were talking about putting feet to our faith. In some ways, a lot of our people felt their faith was just an intellectual exercise, saying they believed in God but not showing it. So they welcomed the chance to get involved in something practical. We all did."

"Wait till you hear everything they've done in five years, Nikki," Marta said.

"Marta knows I'm pretty pleased about this. So far we've sponsored five families—sometimes we do more than one at a time. It's taken a couple years to get each of them settled. And we've also been involved in less comprehensive projects, like just finding work or housing or sponsors, for about 20 other immigrants from right on the other side of our own border with Mexico. And you're right, Nikki, it is a lot of work. But it's hard to tell who benefits more—the people we help or us. God changes us both in the process."

He pulled a pack of cinnamon gum from his pocket and

offered it to both of them. "Marta told me you just became a Christian recently," he said to Nikki.

She nodded, unwrapping her stick of gum. "Yeah, not even a month ago." She stopped there, but Ted raised his bushy eyebrows and waited, so she continued. "I don't know how much Aunt Marta told you. I guess it's no secret that this has been a pretty wild year for me. I, uh, I got pregnant last spring, and the baby was born the end of January." *Why are you doing this? I thought you weren't gonna tell this to anybody out here!* she thought. But telling Ted seemed different somehow, and she went on.

"I made up my mind that I needed to place the baby for adoption, so he could have a real family, you know? But after he was born, it turned out to be a lot harder to do than I'd expected. I almost changed my mind."

She stopped and looked out across the water. The sun, which had been reflecting brightly off the blue expanse, seemed to dim a bit, and Nikki watched the little whitecaps peak here and there.

"So what happened?" Ted asked gently.

Nikki looked up and met his brown eyes with her own. She saw interest there, and compassion, and she could see why he and Marta were such good friends. *He's as easy to talk to as she is,* Nikki thought. Usually, she kept these things to herself, sharing them only when she absolutely had to, but talking to Ted was so comfortable that she didn't hesitate.

"I decided in the end that it would be best for Evan—that's the baby's name—to go ahead with the adoption. I just wasn't sure how I would get through it. But when the pastor at the adoption ceremony started talking about God loving us the way we love our children, and about how He wants to adopt us into His family, then things started to make sense—things

Aunt Marta and my grandparents had been saying for years, and stuff that Jeff Allen, a really good friend of mine, had been telling me, too. It was like God was right there with me, telling me how much He loved me and that He would forgive me, so I let Him. And all of a sudden, I knew He was helping me do what I needed to do—give Evan to his new family."

Ted chewed his gum silently for a minute, then asked, "And how are you doing with everything now?"

Nikki took a deep breath. "Well, I feel like that part of my life—about the baby, I mean—is settled now. I'll always love Evan and pray for him every day. And I get to see him every six months, according to the adoption agreement. But as for the rest of my life, I feel like I lost almost a whole year. While everyone else at school was figuring out what colleges to apply to and what they wanted to do with their lives, I was picking a home for my baby, you know? So I need to get busy with that. And—I'm just—kind of, well, starting to figure out what it means to live like a Christian."

Ted laughed. "I can relate to you there. I've been a Christian for 15 years now, and sometimes I still feel like I'm just starting to figure it out! Seriously, though, maybe you'd like to get together and talk about things while you're out here, especially since I hear you have some time on your hands with Marta so busy with the conference."

"Thanks, Ted. I think I might like that," Nikki said, surprising herself. *It's because he gives you this feeling that you really matter to him,* she thought. *I could probably tell him some of the things MacKenzie said that have really bothered me.*

Nikki's thoughts were interrupted as the ship's whistle blew twice in the prearranged signal for everyone to return to the boat. Marta looked up in surprise.

"We haven't been here that long, have we?" A sudden shiver ran through her as she ended her sentence.

Ted frowned and looked upward. "I expect it has something to do with the fog moving in." He pointed to the mountains that formed the spine of the island, and they could see long fingers of white fog streaming down each slope, outlining valleys and crevices Nikki hadn't even noticed before. "And it explains why you're shivering, too."

He pulled off the sweat jacket knotted around his waist and offered it to Marta. "If the fog is moving in that fast, then we'd better get back to the boat pretty quick." He reached down for the blanket and gave it a shake before he folded it quickly and stuffed it into his backpack. "See what I mean about the weather, Nik? When the fog rolls in thick and fast like this, a little sloop like mine can get trapped out here." He saw the startled look in Nikki's eyes and added, "But don't worry—the *Suncatcher*'s much faster than my boat. We'll have plenty of time to get back to Santa Linnea before the fog comes in."

Nikki was counting steps as she began the long descent toward the dock. She'd started counting for fun, then decided it was boring and tried to stop, but her mind seemed to go on announcing numbers in rhythm with her footsteps: *263, 264, 265 . . .*

"I have a feeling I'm going to have to spend the whole day in the Jacuzzi at the hotel tomorrow, I'll be so sore," she laughed when they reached the bottom, then noticed that neither Ted nor Marta was listening to her.

They were looking to the left, in the direction of the cave, and Nikki's glance followed theirs. The tide was all the way out now, and the sandy floor of the cave, littered with the usual bits of shells and mounded clumps of brown-green kelp covered with flies, now held signs as well—large, hand-lettered signs affixed to wooden poles and stuck upright into the ground. Her sore muscles forgotten, Nikki hurried to get closer to the mouth of the cave with Ted and Marta.

OFF-LIMITS FOR EXPERIMENTS!
KEEP THE ISLANDS FOR OUR CHILDREN!
NOW AND ALWAYS—HANDS OFF THE ISLANDS!

Nikki read the signs, then looked up at the people standing on one of the broad, flat ledges in the back of the cave, their arms linked, chanting loudly, "Preserve, not profit," and realized with a start that MacKenzie was one of them.

Even there, 30 feet above the floor of the cave, MacKenzie stood out from the dozen or so people around her. On either side of her were the students Nikki had seen with her on the boat, and she seemed to be in charge of them. Nikki watched in amazement. *I could never do something like that. But it's not hard for MacKenzie. She always seems to know exactly what she's doing, and she's always sure her way is right. I wonder what it takes to come up with that kind of superconfidence?*

Several tourists crowded closer, snapping pictures and pointing video recorders at the demonstrators just as they had at the seals and the dolphins. The boat's captain tried to wave them away, then started arguing with the demonstrators, standing in the mouth of the cave while gesturing toward the *Suncatcher* and the fog advancing down the mountainsides.

"Look, we need to get out of here *now*," he was shouting angrily. "The fog will cover everything within the next half hour. What do you expect me to do? Put a whole boatload of passengers in danger just because you want to make a point?"

The demonstrators yelled back at him, their words jumbled together as several of them spoke over one another. The only word Nikki could catch was *press*.

"We can't *wait* for some news guy to get you on film," the captain shouted. "Now I'm real sorry if that messes up your plans to be on the six o'clock news, but I have a *job* to do here, you understand? Now get back on the boat!"

The demonstrators didn't budge.

"Fine. That's just fine." He threw up his hands, disgusted. "I'll call the coast guard, and you can sit here in the fog and wait for them. You know they'll haul you away by force if they have to. This is government land." There was no answer, and he tried again. "Listen, if you don't get back on the boat now, I can't be responsible for what happens to you." He waited a second, then turned on one heel and started walking back toward the boat. As he passed Nikki, she could hear him muttering ". . . crazy treehuggers. Next I'll have Greenpeace boarding my tours."

There was a commotion behind where Nikki stood, and she turned to see the TV cameraman pushing his way to the front of the spectators. Immediately, MacKenzie pointed him out and started to position the other demonstrators to make sure each sign could be clearly seen.

In just the few minutes they'd been standing there, Nikki noticed that the fog had already covered the high meadow where they had been sitting. The mountains that formed the middle of the island were completely shrouded now, and the day took on a gray and brooding look. Nikki shivered at the clammy feel of the foggy air on her bare arms.

"What's the issue here, anyway?" she asked, rubbing her

arms to try to warm them. "I don't even understand what's going on."

"It's the battle between the oil companies and the environmentalists that Alex told us about, remember?" Marta answered.

Ted stood with his hands in the pockets of his gray shorts, arms pressed against his sides, and tried to squelch a shiver that ran through him. "There's a lot of oil beneath these waters, and the oil companies are chomping at the bit to get at it. On the other hand, the environmentalists are enraged that they would even consider moving in on one of the country's largest wildlife preserves."

"It does sound kind of surprising," Marta put in. "I mean, think what one oil spill would do to all those elephant seals and the pelicans and all. . . ."

"That's why they're demonstrating," Ted said. "I think the only reason the oil companies' request is even being considered is that they've said they'd help patrol the area for drug activities."

"That's what Alex was telling us."

"But the environmentalists won't even *talk* about it," Ted said.

Nikki watched him closely as he stared with narrowed eyes at MacKenzie's group. There was a twinge of disgust in his voice, and it puzzled her. "Why do you disagree with what they're doing?" she asked.

He swung around to face her, and his usually mild brown eyes flashed. "Disagree? I *don't* disagree, Nikki, not with trying to preserve the islands as a wildlife sanctuary."

"What then?"

Ted pursed his lips and was silent for a moment before he

answered. "Let's just say I'm not real sure of the motives of the person, or persons, behind this demonstration."

Nikki wanted to ask more, but the boat whistle sounded again. Ted turned and offered Marta his arm and led them back toward the dock. The crew members began urging people to hurry aboard.

"What about MacKenzie?" Nikki asked as she stepped off the gangplank and onto the deck. "Will they get caught here in the fog?"

Ted shook his head. "If you watch, I think you'll see them make a dash to get back on board at the very last minute—*after* they've gotten all the TV exposure possible."

Marta went to search for the extra sweatshirts and jackets they had shed earlier, but Nikki stayed at the railing with Ted as the boat engines began to throb once again and the crew members prepared to pull up the gangplank. At the last possible minute, the demonstrators did exactly what Ted had predicted. They clambered down from the ledge and pulled up their signs from the floor of the cave, then made a dash for the boat. The TV cameraman ran backward in front of them as long as he could, shooting footage all the way, and still made it on board.

But by the time MacKenzie's group reached the boat, it had already begun to move away from the dock. The demonstrators stood on shore, demanding that they be allowed aboard, but from where Nikki stood beside Ted, she could see the captain's flushed face in the wheelhouse above the deck. He shook his head angrily and kept the boat pulling away, the space between the deck and the dock widening.

Nikki shot a glance upward. Very little of the island remained visible now, and she blew a breath out in a low, whistling sound. "Are we just gonna *leave* them here?"

Ted gave a wry grin and raised his eyebrows. "I doubt it, Nikki. Something tells me that MacKenzie's a better politician than that."

Nikki looked back at the demonstrators in time to see MacKenzie gesturing to the cameraman, first gesturing at the video camera, then at the group around her, then at the boat. Her words were inaudible now, but her point was clear.

The cameraman quickly started to shoot footage of the demonstrators, now looking suitably upset, and of the departing boat. Then he swung his camera upward in a tight shot of the wheelhouse.

Nikki thought she may never before have seen such a look of fury as the one that crossed the captain's face when he realized he'd be seen on the six o'clock news stranding a bedraggled group of demonstrators on the fog-shrouded dock.

For a long, tense second, nothing happened, then she felt the motors cut back as the boat stopped, then began to pull back alongside the dock.

Ted looked down at Nikki and winked. "What'd I tell you?"

Ten

THE NEXT MORNING, which was Sunday, Nikki and her aunt barely got up on time to make the short drive down the coast to the church Ted pastored. The boat ride home from Andaluca in the fog had taken four hours instead of two, and by the time they got a pizza for dinner and fell into bed, they were exhausted.

"You're telling me you didn't even *hear* the alarm?" Nikki asked for a second time, trying to imagine her aunt, who usually reacted instantly and violently to any loud sound in the morning, sleeping through the alarm.

"Well," Marta said, looking slightly embarrassed, "I do have a faint memory of it. *Very* faint. I think I reached over and hit the clock radio, and it just never came back on." The car topped a slight rise, and Marta pointed at the expansive ocean view as she continued. "Anyway, what about *you*? I don't recall you even budging."

Nikki grinned. "Yeah, but, Aunt Marta, what else would you expect from me?"

"True," Marta said, grinning back.

Nikki watched the incredible ocean vista silently for a few minutes, then asked, "How'd you meet Ted, anyway?"

"Back in college, when Ted and I were both freshmen, we worked together to get an InterVarsity group started on campus," Marta answered. "And things just sort of—went on—from there."

"Went on?"

"Yes, Nikki! The friendship *went on*. It continued. I see him a few times a year."

"Well, he's obviously head over heels about you. He's got a boat, he's got a good job, he lives in a gorgeous part of the country—think about never having to see snow again! So what's keeping this, uh, *friendship* from turning into something else?"

Nikki expected a quick, sassy reply, but to her surprise, Marta drove silently for a mile or more before answering. Nikki was just about to repeat her question when Marta finally spoke, quietly.

"Because, in the end, love isn't so much about what he can give me as it is about what I can give *him*. And I'm still not sure about that."

She spoke so soberly that Nikki knew her aunt had spent a great deal of time mulling the question over. *So*, she thought, *I guess that's the end of that conversation, at least for now.*

Ted—or Reverend Wilcox, as the bulletin referred to him—turned out to look much less impressive on the platform than he did in his deck shoes and shorts. Nikki had to hold back a grin as she watched him walk to the pulpit in a suit that was a little too baggy and a tie that made her cringe. *Good thing I got to know him before I saw him this way,* she thought. She slid her eyes sideways, checking out the people around her, but no one else acted amused.

"You all know that 'faith,'" Ted began, "'is the substance of things hoped for, the evidence of things not seen,' as Hebrews tells us. And a mighty important substance, too, I'd say, since the Bible tells us no person can see God without it. Let me read you a statement by a well-known twentieth-century Christian, C. S. Lewis."

A subdued chuckle rippled through the congregation, and Ted paused and looked up, then grinned apologetically. "Not surprised, huh? I admit, he's an author I quote a lot. But he has a knack for saying hard things in a simple way."

Nikki looked around, more openly this time. She could see by the smiles on the faces around her and the gentle sound of their laughter that this man had somehow won the right to say nearly anything he wanted to these people.

At first, it was hard for Nikki to concentrate, thinking as she was about how she would change Ted, if she had a magic wand, so that he could capture Marta's full attention. She scrutinized his tie, the shiny top of his head, and thought, *You'd have to be a lot more aggressive, more of a "take charge" kind of guy, to get my aunt's attention.* Her mind flashed back suddenly to the end of the airplane flight and their meeting with Lee Tierney. The picture of Marta's face, rapt and intent on everything Lee said while he exuded charm, was very clear.

Nikki studied Ted again and shook her head slightly. *I don't think there's any way you can beat him out, Ted.*

"What's wrong?" Marta's whisper was insistent, concerned. "Why?"

"Because you're sitting there shaking your head."

"Sorry!" Nikki answered. She pulled herself up straighter in the hard pew, determined to pay attention.

Ted was intent on what he was saying, and suddenly, her thoughts about his tie got lost in the shadow of his words, which seemed to be addressed directly to her. "Lewis says, 'Faith . . . is the art of holding on to things your reason has once accepted, in spite of your changing moods. For moods will change, whatever view your reason takes.'"

Nikki thought immediately of the conflict she'd felt listening to MacKenzie in the office on Friday.

"Lewis goes on to describe how each of us who is a believer has times, or moods, when Christianity looks improbable. But then he adds that, when he was an atheist, he had times when *atheism* looked very improbable. 'This rebellion of your moods against your real self is going to come anyway,' he says. The point is, everybody has doubts."

Nikki couldn't help answering him in her mind. *I can show you one person who doesn't, Ted. MacKenzie's probably the queen of confidence!*

"Moods change," Ted continued. "Lewis's conclusion is that we have to learn to control our moods, and in order to do that, we must continually and regularly feed our faith by means of prayer and reading, both the Scriptures and writings of other Christians about the Scriptures. Lewis says, 'We have to be continually reminded of what we believe. Neither this belief nor any other will automatically remain alive in the mind.' And I would add that we must never forget that Christianity is a relationship, not simply agreeing with a set of rules."

Maybe I'm not the only one who's struggled with doubts! That thought alone gave Nikki courage. She listened to every sentence that followed, right up to the end of the sermon, when Ted quoted another author, Oswald Chambers.

"'Faith is not intelligent understanding, faith is deliberate commitment to a Person where I see no way.'"

The sun shone brilliantly on the drive back to the hotel, and they could see for miles up and down the curving coastline. Nikki watched the green palms and bright fuchsia clusters of bougainvillea flash past the car windows and listened to Ted's words, "Moods change," echo in her ears.

"Aunt Marta?" she asked finally.

"Yes?"

"Can I ask you something?"

"Of course."

"Do you ever have—well, you know, doubts? Like Ted was talking about?"

Marta didn't hesitate. "Absolutely. Both Ted and I struggled with that, especially back in college. That's why he's so good on the subject—he knows what he's talking about from experience." She glanced across the front seat at her niece. "I think he's right about the solution, too. Your grandfather gave you a Bible a few weeks ago, right?"

"Yeah." Nikki shrugged and looked down, inspecting her nails. "But you know, sometimes when I read it, it doesn't feel like . . . like I'm getting anything out of it."

"Kind of like eating oatmeal?" Marta asked, and Nikki frowned at her, confused.

"Excuse me? What's oatmeal got to do with this?"

"Well, you may need help learning how to study the Bible, and I can list a bunch of good ways to do it that have helped me.

But the bottom line—" Marta checked the mirrors and glanced over her left shoulder, then switched lanes smoothly "—is that people don't have a spiritual high every single time they read the Bible, no matter what they tell you. Just as you may not get especially excited about eating oatmeal every morning. But if you *do* eat it, whether it's dressed up with peaches and cream or whether it's just plain old oatmeal, the truth is, you'll have energy for just about whatever you want to do that morning."

Nikki shook her head. "Uh, I'm not making the connection here. Sorry."

"Some days, reading the Bible is a great experience in itself, like eating oatmeal with peaches and cream. But other days, while it may not seem very exciting, it still gets you all stoked up for what's coming, like eating plain old oatmeal. Which part are you reading, Nik?"

"I just started at the beginning, at Genesis."

Marta grinned. "Oh, great. So now you're into the 'begats'? Those lists of who had what kid?"

Nikki nodded. "Exactly!"

"Well, I'm sorry we didn't talk about this earlier. I've been so busy thinking about this conference and—anyway, that doesn't matter now. You might try starting with John, in the New Testament. There's absolutely nothing wrong with Genesis, I'm not saying that, but you might want to start out just a little easier. And maybe read a psalm and a proverb every day, too. And then you could work on memorizing some of it, so it's always there in your head when you need it."

After lunch in the hotel dining room, they returned to their room, and Marta spread papers and books all over the desk, then switched on her laptop.

"Time for me to get to work. In exactly three days, I have to read this paper to a few hundred of the most educated people I know, so it would be nice if I could sound at least a *little* scholarly."

"Don't want the real truth to get out, huh?" Nikki asked, then laughed when Marta peered at her over the top of her glasses and the vertical lines appeared between her eyebrows.

"Nikki, didn't you tell me you had something really important to do? Like go lie by the pool?"

"I'm going, I'm going!" Nikki said, laughing as she wriggled into shorts and slid her feet into sandals. "Just let me get decent first, okay?"

"Well, you certainly have my permission to do that," Marta said absently, switching the desk lamp off and on with no results. She bent forward and peered underneath the metal shade, then unscrewed the lightbulb and shook it gently. There was a tinkling rattle from the glass tube. "Oh, brother. I think this bulb's blown. Nik, would you mind asking somebody at the desk to send up another bulb when you go downstairs?"

"No problem," Nikki answered, taking one last look at her hair in the mirror and wondering idly if Antonio might be working today. She left then, pulling the door shut behind her.

The colorful profusion of flowers and turquoise water of the pool were almost blinding in the midday sun. Nikki slipped on her sunglasses and lay back in the padded lounge chair, letting her skin soak up the welcome warmth. She dozed off for a few minutes, her muscles lulled by the heat, but soon the rattle of a cleaning cart and the staccato Spanish voices of the maids woke her.

She listened, trying to make sense of the Spanish, but it

was hopeless. They spoke so fast that she caught perhaps one word out of 10. *Great,* she thought. *Two years of Spanish and a million vocabulary lists, and I still can't understand a simple, every-day conversation.* The sun had moved far enough that its rays fell directly on her face, and Nikki squeezed her eyes tightly shut, even behind sunglasses. The brightness of the light reminded her, and she sat up suddenly. Somehow, between the room and the pool, she'd forgotten completely about Aunt Marta's lightbulb.

She swung her legs over the side of the lounge chair and turned around to face the maids. "Do you know where I could find a maintenance worker named Antonio?" she asked.

The two women looked at her, then at each other.

"Antonio," Nikki said again, slowly and clearly.

One of the women spread her hands, palms up, in front of her and shook her head back and forth vigorously.

Great, Nikki thought. *Now I have to do this in Spanish, and my accent will probably make them both die laughing.* She hesitated a moment, trying to remember the right sound to give the vowels, then said slowly, "¿Donde está Antonio?"

Her worst fears came true. The younger woman giggled, and the other smiled broadly. This time, they shook their heads in unison.

Nikki opened her mouth to say "gracias" but decided against more humiliation and simply smiled her thanks. She pulled her shorts and shirt back on over her bathing suit, then turned and went through the sliding doors to the lobby and waited while the desk clerk chatted, his back toward her, on the phone for several minutes. He sat backward on his chair, long legs straddling the seat, leafing through a magazine spread open on the desk as he talked. When at last Nikki cleared her throat, he glanced over his shoulder, covered the receiver with one hand, and raised his eyebrows.

She explained about the lightbulb and asked if he could have a new one sent up to room 223. He nodded, still listening all the while to the phone, scrawled the room number across the top margin of the magazine page, gave Nikki a quick thumbs-up sign, and went back to his conversation.

Nikki stood still a second, then cleared her throat again, more pointedly this time. The clerk glanced back at her and sighed.

"Hang on," he said into the mouthpiece, then looked at her with some annoyance.

"Do you—uh, do you happen to have a guy who works here named Antonio? In maintenance?"

"Look, we have a million Mexicans on our payroll. How would I—?"

A smartly dressed young woman with hair as black as Antonio's walked out of the back office just then and stepped up to the front counter. She wore a badge that displayed her name and the word *Manager.* The desk clerk jerked upright, suddenly attentive.

The dark-haired woman smiled politely at Nikki. "We have no one on our payroll named Antonio. Is there something else I can do for you?"

"No," Nikki said. "No, but thank you."

❧ *Eleven* ❧

NIKKI TURNED AND LEFT THE LOBBY, grabbing an apple from the fruit bowl as she passed, and made her way outside to the beach. Her mind was swirling with questions, and she began walking along the shore without thinking much about where she was going.

She settled her sunglasses over her eyes and headed toward the cliffs where she'd met Antonio, his words about the stone bridge flashing through her mind. Upon hearing that he didn't work at the hotel at all, curiosity burned inside her. Why had he been so intent on steering her back toward the hotel and away from the arch?

He'd acted as though he was concerned for her safety, but now, picturing his face when he spoke, Nikki knew there had been more in his eyes and voice than that.

So what's he hiding? Why doesn't he want me over there?

As soon as she thought the words, Nikki laughed at herself. *Cloak-and-dagger,* she mocked herself again, and began mentally composing an answer to Jeff's E-mail question. *You may be right, Jeff. I just may be getting bored. Bored enough to start seeing mysteries where there's probably a perfectly good explanation.*

The hot afternoon sand burned the edges of her feet as it trickled into the sides of her sandals, and she leaned down and slipped them off, dangling them from each hand as she veered closer to the surf and chased the edges of the waves back and forth.

She tried to force her mind to concentrate on the shells and pelicans, the cormorants and sanderlings, but her thoughts kept returning to Antonio. Soon she realized her feet were taking her closer and closer to the stone bridge.

All Antonio's quiet words about cormorants and dolphins and loving the ocean seemed suspect now. *Good job again, Nik. As usual, you fell for a line,* she told herself. Would she ever learn how to tell if people could be trusted or not? She walked faster, angry at herself for being taken in. *The problem with you is, you get taken in by any guy who's good-looking.* Antonio's dark, intense eyes and his easy, unconscious charm had caught her attention, she had to admit.

When she reached the first bluff and crossed its flat top to look over into the hidden cove, Nikki was relieved to see that the tide was out. She stood staring at the stone arch and the cavern, now empty of water. It would be no problem to get to the next cliff now. She could make her way down the path that ran diagonally across the side of the cliff, then cross the wet, sandy bottom and climb the path on the other side.

Or, the thought trickled into her mind, *you could cross the bridge. It'd be easy now, with no rushing water underneath to make you lose your balance.*

Nikki eyed the bridge. The thought of starting across it

gave her the same kind of butterflies-in-the-stomach feeling she'd gotten for a few minutes on the *Suncatcher,* out in the shipping lanes. She hesitated a moment more, then turned and started down the path away from the bridge.

Before long, she reached the top of the next cliff, and she stood to take in the view of the private cove. She could see from here how, even at low tide, the cove was cut off from the rest of the beach by the two long cliffs that formed its boundaries, the one behind her and the one a half mile up the beach. They reached all the way to the water on both sides like arms stretched out to enclose it.

From this vantage point, Nikki could see that the ruined building tilted at a crazy angle over the edge of the cliff had once been a house. Two window frames with the glass missing stared like dark, empty eyes out at the ocean. Farther down the cliff were the tumbled remains of a redwood deck, its wood supports buckled from the force of whatever disaster had destroyed this home.

Alex's voice echoed in her mind. *"The beach areas were hit hard, too. We lost a couple gorgeous homes that were built too close to the cliffs."*

Behind the ruined house was a small outbuilding that still stood intact near the very edge of the cliff. It looked like an extra garage, though larger than usual. *Probably for a boat,* she thought. Around it, the long, fingerlike leaves of the tall eucalyptus grove waved in the breeze with dry, shuffling noises, and Nikki could smell their sharp fragrance mixed with the faint fish scent of the ocean air.

Around the outskirts of what had been a yard were azalea bushes and more bougainvillea, sprawling over everything in reach, their flowers a splash of bright pink and

fuchsia. It was overgrown and unkempt, and the deserted-
ness of it depressed her.

So why was Antonio so anxious to keep me away from this?
Why should he care if she saw the bridge or the boathouse or
anything else here? She had just made up her mind to turn
back in the direction of the hotel when there was a moment of
stillness in the rhythm of the waves and the flickering breeze.
And in that stillness, she heard a voice.

Nikki stopped dead and listened. Another wave crashed
on the shore far below and the eucalyptus leaves shuffled in
the wind again, but Nikki stood like a statue, her head cocked,
waiting. It came again—the high, thin voice of a child.

She swung around. There, behind the band of eucalyptus
trees where Nikki stood, a tiny dark-haired girl whirled
around and around in the center of the small grove. She held
her thin, brown arms out straight to either side and spun like
a top, her delicate bare feet flying faster and faster over the
green grass until the skirt of her sundress opened out around
her like a pink umbrella.

Nikki grinned, remembering how she'd spun around that
way when she was little, how her breath grew short and her
spinning became slower and slower, just as the little girl's
was now. At last the child wobbled and sank cross-legged to
the grass, still swaying back and forth slightly for another
minute, staring up, and Nikki knew from experience that the
tall trees were still spinning before her eyes. After a few seconds, she bent and picked up a gray, lumpy-looking doll with
a red dress from the grass and hugged it tight against her side
with one hand. With the other, she pointed up at the eucalyptus trees towering overhead, then turned her head toward
the doll and appeared to speak to it.

Nikki crept a few steps closer. The only word she recognized was *mariposa,* and she searched her mind, then remembered it meant "butterfly." *At last,* she thought. *All those vocabulary lists in Spanish, and I can recognize one whole word!*

Nikki listened again and realized with surprise that the child was singing. She held the doll as high as her short arms would allow, and Nikki followed her glance to the treetops, then gasped.

Hundreds—maybe thousands—of monarch butterflies clustered on the eucalyptus branches. Hundreds more circled around them. The air was in constant motion as the delicate orange-and-black wings fluttered back and forth. On the branches, where the tiny creatures came to rest in short turns, their wings brushed open and shut, open and shut.

Nikki watched in wonder for several seconds until she heard the song begin again. She glanced back down, taking in the girl's too-thin arms and legs, and the faded pink of the sundress she wore.

What is a child this small doing way out here alone? she wondered, and she felt a familiar tug at her heart. It reminded her of the weeks she'd struggled before she was finally able to hand Evan, her own baby, over to his adoptive parents.

As though in answer to her question, Antonio appeared suddenly at the other side of the grove. Close behind him followed a black-haired man, taller than Antonio by half a foot and sporting a dark mustache that drooped down either side of his full lips. His shoulders were broad and his arms thick in his short-sleeved plaid shirt. His voice, harsh and heavily accented, carried clearly across the grove, and even the little girl ceased her singing and stood frozen as the tension between Antonio and the man seemed to crackle in the air.

Nikki had stopped just in time at the edge of the grove. Another two steps and the trees would not have sheltered her at all, but as it was, she was able to duck quietly behind a huge fallen eucalyptus that had broken in the middle and lay with its large end still attached to the trunk, its top on the ground. From here, she could still see and hear but remain safely out of sight.

Antonio stopped in front of the boathouse, hands on his hips, chin held high, speaking in a voice much louder than he'd used with her. "And if I do not want to be involved in that part of it? I told you I would stand guard for you, but helping you carry it here—" he jerked his head back to the side to indicate the boathouse "—and the diving, that is different." His voice quavered slightly on the last words, and he did not try to correct the thick rolling of his *r*'s as he had with Nikki.

She could see only the back of the taller man now, but she heard his voice ring out. "You have no choice."

"You are wrong," Antonio shot back. "I do have a choice. I will find another job, somehow, till my father gets back."

"Another job?" The older man gave a harsh laugh. "In a country where hiring an illegal is a felony? I think not."

The little girl, obviously feeling the tension, crept close to Antonio, her doll hugged against her chest with one arm. With the other, she reached for his fingers and held on.

Antonio's chin lifted another inch. "Then I will take Mari and go back. To Mexico. I will find him myself."

"You talk like a fool," the man answered. "Marianna is a citizen, the only one of you here legally, and you would take her back across the border? You have paperwork showing she was born here?"

Antonio's lips tightened as he looked down at the child beside him.

"You see?" The man pressed his advantage. "And do you think that, in the future, once you try to return here, your *word* would convince them?" He spat on the ground. "The INS would laugh in your face."

"Then I will go to the courthouse and ask for her papers myself."

"Oh, a fine idea!" The man's voice was thick with scorn. "And they will ask you why you want them and why you should have them. And those will be only the first of many questions, such as where are your mother and father, who should be asking for the papers in the first place. And when they find out your father fled, and *why*, think of the questions you will face then. Like, where is he now? They will expect you to know, Antonio."

The boy swallowed hard and looked away toward the ocean, but the man's voice continued mercilessly. "And then, of course, there is the matter of your papers, or should I say *lack* of papers, that will come to their attention."

Antonio's eyes jerked back toward him. "INS is not that strict with teenagers, I hear. They might understand—"

The harsh laugh sounded again. "Now *there* is a solution," he said derisively. "You live in the past, *paisano*. These days, there is a movement to round up all illegals, to stop paying for the education of their children, to send them back . . . a very strong movement, Antonio. Much stronger than you understand. The only safe way is for you to stay here, do what you are told, and earn the money to bring your father back." The man's voice turned softer, wheedling, and he stepped toward Antonio and put both hands on his shoulders.

Nikki strained to hear.

"You have to let us help you, Antonio. I know the man who leads people over the only safe trail, the only trail the border police have not found yet, and he told me himself he will bring your father back. Perhaps even after this next shipment," he added.

Antonio raised his head and stared into the man's face. "This next one? That's all I would have to help with?" Hope was alive in his face again.

The older man took his hands from Antonio's shoulders and shrugged casually. "Probably. And maybe just a little diving in the future. . . . You are doing well, earning the money quickly. But if you want to see your father back in the United States, you have no choice." He stepped backward. "I have to go now."

Nikki pressed back into the foliage of the fallen tree. *Please, Lord, don't let him see me.* Then she stopped short as the man began to leave.

Antonio seemed to gather his courage together, and he called out, "For me, this *is* the last time." The man stopped dead, not 10 feet from where Nikki hid. He turned slowly, deliberately, and she could see the hardness in his dark eyes.

"Is that so?"

Antonio flinched, then stiffened his back and gave one short, sharp nod with his head.

One side of the man's mouth turned up, and he glanced down at the little girl who had her face buried in the denim of Antonio's jeans. He crouched down and clicked his tongue so that she whirled around to look at him and found his face on her level. "Come here. Come. Don't be afraid. Herrera-Ortiz does not hurt children." He stretched out his hand, and she stepped hesitantly toward him.

Antonio took a step after her, but Herrera-Ortiz held up one hand, fingers wide apart. "Why do you fear? Your father and I were good friends. Do you think I would hurt his child, his Marianna? I even know the special name he had for her, after the little song she sings, the one about the butterflies. Come here, *Mariposa.*"

Antonio stopped, and his hands hung limply at his sides as though he was unsure what to do next.

"Come, *mi hija.* Come here." Marianna stepped to his side, her eyes trusting. The man reached down and gathered her into his arms, lifting her face to his, and as he did, the doll slipped from her grasp.

She wailed, reaching toward the ground, straining after it.

The man gave a gentle laugh, and Nikki relaxed a little. He straightened up with the doll in one hand and Mari in the other arm. She was still reaching for it, but he held it just out of her grasp and spoke directly to her with a wide smile on his face, though Nikki felt a chill of fear at the sudden sinister quality of his voice and knew immediately that his words were meant for Antonio's ears.

"Such a pretty child, such a pretty, pretty, *beautiful* child. The pride and joy of the family, that is what you are, Marianna."

She stretched out both arms, wiggling and squirming, struggling to reach her treasure.

But Herrera-Ortiz loosened his grasp and slid her to the ground, then took the doll in both hands.

"Such a pretty doll," he began in the same tones he had used about the little girl, his smile still wide as he spoke. "Such a *beautiful* doll." Then he deliberately inserted his finger in the neck of the doll's dress and pulled. The flimsy red dress tore down the front so that it hung in two pieces, and he looked directly at Antonio. "Now she is not so beautiful, eh?"

He tossed the doll to the ground in front of the girl, turned on his heel, and strode off, disappearing through the trees. There was the sound of an engine starting somewhere beyond the grove, followed by the screech of a vehicle roaring away.

Nikki felt like someone had punched her in the stomach, knocking all the breath out of her, and she swayed for a moment, unsteady, trying to get it back.

What finally made it possible for her to move again was the sight of the little girl squatting in the dusty grass beside the doll. Her faded pink sundress sagged between her thin knees, and she reached out one tiny finger and touched the doll timidly, then stood up and looked at Antonio, as if she expected him to fix it.

Antonio, however, didn't move. His cheeks were flushed and his breathing fast as he stared at the doll.

Tears slid from the child's eyes, marking a clear trail down her dusty cheeks. *If anybody ever made Evan cry like that, I'd—* Then Marianna sobbed, and Nikki forgot all about the fact that she was supposed to be hiding. She stepped out from her shelter behind the fallen eucalyptus and started toward the child. A dry twig crackled beneath her sandal, and Antonio's head snapped up at the sound.

It was a long time before Nikki could erase from her mind the look of sheer panic on Antonio's face when he saw her.

❧ Twelve ❧

ANTONIO'S CHEST HEAVED up and down with each breath, and it was obvious that for a minute he could not speak. Marianna picked up the doll and moved back to Antonio's side, curling one arm tightly around his knee and once again hiding her face against the denim of his jeans, squashing the doll between them.

Nikki could see she'd scared both of them, though Antonio struggled to mask the panic that had flashed across his face. She opened her mouth to speak, then stopped. How was she supposed to explain her presence? "I was spying on you"? Or, "I found out you lied about working at the hotel, and it made me curious"? Or maybe, "I wanted to know why you tried to keep me away from here, so I came snooping around"?

She had to say something. Nikki cleared her throat and tried to sound casual. "Uh, I was just out taking a walk and . . ."

Her words seemed to unfreeze Antonio. He turned and spoke over her to the little girl. "Mari, go inside. Stay there till I call you."

The child moved swiftly to the boathouse and disappeared inside the door. Then Antonio took a step closer to Nikki. "Why did you come here?"

"That's what I was trying to tell you. I was taking a walk—"

"No one walks this direction since the rains washed away so much of the cliffs." His words were stiff and precise, and she could tell he was trying hard to keep the accent out of his voice, struggling not to roll his *r*'s. "Everyone knows they are dangerous. I told you that before."

"Well, I'm new here." She felt defensive, and she could hear the angry tinge in her words. "I didn't mean to spy on you. I was just walking, and I heard Mari—is that what you called her?"

"Yes. She is my sister."

"Well, I heard her singing, and I was afraid a child could get hurt, playing way out here all by herself."

He stared at her, his eyes narrowed.

"So I stopped to see what was going on." Nikki's glance took in the wrecked house, the overgrown, unkempt yard beneath the eucalyptus trees, and Antonio's gray T-shirt that strained across his chest and shoulders, the same shirt he'd been wearing the other two days she'd seen him.

"And you and that man walked up just then, so I stayed hidden behind the tree over there." Nikki stopped and waited for his reply, but Antonio said nothing. He just kept staring at her, his face dark with fury. "Well, what'd you expect me to do, come out and introduce myself in front of him?"

Antonio stuffed his hands into his pockets and muttered two angry, short words in Spanish, words Nikki was sure had never been on any of her vocabulary lists. *This is a first,* she thought. *For once I'm glad I can't translate.*

"I'm sorry, Antonio. I didn't mean to eavesdrop. I just didn't know what else to do, so I hid."

Antonio blew a long sigh through pursed lips, and his face relaxed a little. "I understand." He hesitated, then looked into her eyes. "I am sorry, I cannot remember your name."

"Nikki. Nikki Sheridan." Now it was her turn to hesitate, but she had to say something. "I was just going to leave, but when I saw what that man did to the doll, I had to do something. See, I could fix it for her, sew the dress back together. . . ." Her voice trailed off under his intent gaze, and she heard herself adding, "Unless you know someone else who could do it, that is."

His face softened, and she could see she'd caught him off guard. "Thank you. My sister—Marianna—she loves the doll, you can see. My mother made it for her."

"Oh," Nikki said, "then your mother will probably want to fix it herself."

"No." His eyes went bleak, closed down. "My mother is—not alive anymore."

Nikki stopped, searching her mind for something appropriate to say. "Oh, Antonio, I'm sorry." Then the image of the man Antonio had been arguing with flashed across her mind. What was it he had said? *"If you want to see your father back in the United States, you have no choice."*

The picture of Antonio in the hotel lobby, stuffing bagels and fruit in the pockets of his jacket, began to make more sense. There were a million other questions swirling around in Nikki's mind, but she asked only one, glancing at the boathouse. "You don't *live* here, do you?"

Antonio shook his head. "Of course not," he said, his voice

defensive. "I told you before, we live back there—" he nodded back toward town, in the direction she'd heard the truck disappear "—by the airport." She wondered again if he meant the shacks she'd seen when she and Marta first left the airport, but Antonio was still talking. "I come here to do work, odd jobs, for that man you saw. It is just until my father returns. I have other jobs, too. I help the people who live near me, the older ones who do not speak English, with their papers, their job applications."

She nodded, holding back the first comment that came to mind—that she hoped these jobs were a whole lot more real than the one he'd mentioned at the hotel. Over Antonio's shoulder, a movement caught her eye. The boathouse door eased open a few inches, and Mari peeped around its edge, her dark eyes wide as she stared at Nikki.

Antonio gave a short sigh, his face troubled. "Nikki, I must ask you, please do not tell anyone you saw us here. I will have . . . trouble . . . if you give us away."

Nikki shrugged. "I don't even know anybody in this town to tell. But, Antonio, if there's some way I could help . . ."

He stared at her for a moment, then lifted his chin and started to shake his head back and forth. Nikki was afraid she had offended him, but all he said was, "The only help we need is that you not tell anyone. But thank you."

"I guess I'll get going then." Nikki stuck her hands back into the pockets of her shorts and started to turn, but her right hand touched the cool smoothness of the apple from the hotel lobby. Her fingers closed around it quickly, and she called his name. When he turned, she held the fruit out to him. "For Marianna."

The shed door flew all the way open so that it hit the wall behind it with a bang, and before Antonio could grasp the apple, the little girl stood beside him, one arm hugging the doll, the small fingers of her other hand outstretched toward the fruit.

Nikki crouched down till she was eye-level with the girl. The child's round eyes were wide and shining, as dark as her brother's, and thickly fringed with long lashes. She held the tip of her tongue between her small white teeth, as if waiting to see whether this stranger would make good on her offer. Nikki handed her the apple, and the little girl swung around to face her brother, holding her prize high for his inspection. "¡Mira, Antonio! ¡Manzana!" She giggled, a high, happy sound, then crunched into the fruit.

Antonio smiled then, too. "She loves apples. Thank you again." He swung his sister up into his arms and settled her on his hip. "Say thank you, Mari. Say thank you to Nikki."

The child, suddenly shy, hid her face against his chest, but Antonio continued to urge her to respond. Finally, muffled against his T-shirt, came a mumbled "gracias."

"No, say it in English. Come on."

Instead, Mari held the apple up to his mouth, offering him a bite.

He took a small bite and nodded at her, smiling. "Good. Very good, Mari. Thank you."

"Would you like me to take the doll with me? The hotel puts those little sewing kits in everyone's room, and I could fix it tonight."

Antonio watched his sister chewing happily as he considered Nikki's question. "I do not think she could go to sleep without it."

"Then how about if I come back tomorrow? Will you be working here then?"

Antonio nodded. "In the morning I will."

"Fine. I'll bring the sewing stuff and fix it here." Nikki said good-bye and started back.

When she reached the hotel room, she opened the door slowly, trying not to disturb Marta. But her aunt was oblivious. Thin, reedy strains of music escaped the headphones of her portable CD player—just loud enough for Nikki to recognize Ralph Vaughan William's Fifth Symphony. The gold-shaded desk lamp, in working order once again, illuminated the papers strewn around her, and Marta was typing furiously on her laptop. Nikki grinned, thinking how Gram and Grandpa retreated to the screened-in porch when Marta turned up the volume on her CDs during visits home to their house in Michigan. One of Marta's passions was orchestration, and she had to hear every instrument clearly or she couldn't enjoy the music.

Nikki sprawled across her bed, remote control in hand, and switched on the TV. She found an old movie, one she'd seen before, then thought how luxurious a nap would be. She closed her eyes and tried to sleep but couldn't push Antonio and Mari from her mind. She rolled over and opened her mouth to tell her aunt about them, but Marta's fingers were still flying over the keyboard of the laptop. *I'll tell her later*, Nikki thought, knowing how Marta hated interruptions when she was working.

She closed her eyes again and stretched. The last sound she heard was the overflow from Marta's headphones, the sweet high tones of a violin, and against the back of her eyelids was the picture of little dark-haired Mari whirling around and around beneath the delicate, fluttering cloud of butterflies in the eucalyptus grove.

❧ *Thirteen* ❧

NIKKI WOKE SLOWLY the next morning. A note from her aunt was propped against the desk lamp.

Good morning, Nik!

You were so sound asleep that I didn't want to wake you. I phoned Alex, and she's picking me up on her way to the university, so you have the car for the day if you want to do some sightseeing.

I forgot to tell you last night, but Ted called while you were out yesterday and asked if we would meet him for lunch at the Beach Plum, and I said yes. Hope that's okay with you.

Nikki glanced at the clock radio beside the lamp. It read 9:30, and Nikki flung the covers aside and groaned. There would barely be time to shower and dress before she had to hurry to the cove to fix Marianna's doll. She should never have assumed she'd keep waking up naturally at 6:00 every morning. *Looks like my body got used to Pacific time sooner than I expected.*

As she stood under the steaming water, massaging cherry-scented shampoo into a thick lather with her fingertips, Nikki realized she had dreamed, off and on, about Antonio and Mari and the boathouse all night long.

There had to be some way she could get them some help. Nikki rinsed the suds from her hair and stepped out of the shower, toweling off quickly, and looked at her reflection in the mirror.

Okay, okay, so I promised Antonio I wouldn't tell. But that doesn't mean I can't try to find out what help might be available, does it? It would probably take a whole lot more than just her know-how to figure out a situation like this.

As she stepped into plaid shorts and buttoned her sleeveless shirt, she whispered a prayer. "Lord, I really want to help Antonio and Mari. Could You show me how?" She slipped the hotel sewing kit into the pocket of her shorts, made a quick detour in the lobby to buy a small package of Oreos from a vending machine, and started for the cove.

By the time she reached the boathouse, it was 10:30. Once again, the place looked deserted, and she wondered briefly if Antonio had misled her the day before just to get her to leave.

But when she knocked on the door, there were muffled sounds from inside, as though something was being dragged across the floor, then a rapid-fire burst of Spanish. She could translate enough to know that Antonio was urging his sister to go outside quickly.

Mari opened the door a few inches, holding the doll with

its torn dress, but the minute her eyes met Nikki's, the little girl looked away, in the direction of her feet. Nikki's heart ached to see her in a jumper that was too big for her, with no blouse or shirt underneath. She noticed Marianna's feet were bare again, just before the child closed the door in her face.

Nikki knocked again, and this time Antonio appeared, wiping his hands together to rid them of dust, urging his sister outside. Nikki noticed that he took care not to open the door wide enough for her to see inside the building. An instant later, he shut it carefully behind him.

Nikki sat down on the cement step in front of the door and patted the step beside her, inviting Mari to sit with her. Mari eyed her suspiciously for a moment, then turned and sat at the edge, as far from Nikki as she could get.

Nikki held her hand out for the doll, but Mari pressed it hard against herself, hugging it with both arms.

"Mari," Nikki tried to explain, "I think I can fix it. I could sew it, you know?" She took out the tiny sewing kit and unfolded the cardboard tabs so that all the different colors of thread showed. "See? There's red thread here, enough to fix your doll's dress. If you give her to me, I'll sew her dress back together." She moved her hands as if she were sewing.

Mari looked at her out of the corner of her eye, and Nikki was struck again at the length of those straight, black lashes that seemed to flutter each time she blinked. But her dark brows were drawn together in a line over her eyes, and the corners of her mouth turned down.

Antonio knelt in front of the step and said something rapid in Spanish that Nikki couldn't catch, but that caught Mari's attention. He demonstrated the same sewing motions Nikki had done, and this time she understood. The child looked at her, wide-eyed, and nodded. Someone—Nikki assumed Antonio—had pulled her black hair back into two ponytails, one over each ear, and they bounced up and down as she moved her head. But as soon as she looked back down at the doll, tears started to flow faster than before.

Nikki got to her feet and reached into her shorts pocket for the Oreos. She pulled them out and offered them to Mari.

It would have been comical, if the situation had been different, to see how Mari's tears stopped immediately. She looked back and forth from the cookies to Nikki's face for a second, then threw her arms around Nikki's knees and hugged her.

After that, Mari handed over the doll with ease, busy as she was unwrapping the cookies. She watched and chewed as Nikki laid the doll faceup in her lap and pulled the shredded pieces of red material together till they lined up correctly, then took the first stitch. After the cookies disappeared, Mari lost interest and wandered off into the grove, where Nikki could hear her singing the same song she'd sung the day before.

Antonio took her place on the empty step beside Nikki then. "Thank you for doing this." He leaned forward, his hands folded between his knees.

"No problem. I'm just glad I could help," Nikki answered. She stitched another inch of the torn dress, trying to figure out how to bring up what she wanted to say. Finally, she plunged in. "Antonio? Aren't there some government agencies that would help you and Mari? Like with food and—"

"No!" Antonio sprang to his feet and stared down at her, his eyes burning.

"Hey, calm down!" Nikki said, louder than she meant to because he had startled her. "It was just an idea, okay? I mean, look, I know you must need some help."

"We do not need anything! I am working. I am taking care of Mari."

Nikki looked more intently than she needed to at her sewing. "Antonio, I saw you taking food at the hotel."

There was no answer.

"And the hotel manager says you don't work there at all."

Antonio sighed and stuck both hands into his pockets. Then he sank back down beside Nikki, his shoulders sagging.

"How come you're alone here, anyway?" she asked. "I mean, I know you said your mother died, but . . ."

"What about my father?"

Nikki nodded.

"My father is worse than dead."

"Worse than dead? What does that mean?" Nikki asked.

"One day, two weeks ago, he did not come home from work. He had a job at the university, as a gardener, but then one evening, he never came back. We waited two days to find out what happened."

"Why didn't you just go to the police?" she said. "That's what they're there for."

Antonio made a sound that would have been a laugh if it had had any humor in it. "The police are there for people like you. Not for people like us."

"People like us?"

"This country is for citizens, Nikki. People who belong here. My family came here four years ago, like thousands of people from my country do, with no papers, no sponsors. My mother had one dream for the child she was carrying—that it would be born here, be an American. So we came, and Mari was born in a small town just inside the border. After that, my father had many jobs. He tried to find one that paid enough to support us. I worked with him while my mother stayed with the baby. We picked strawberries, we picked grapes, we picked everything they grow here, all up and down the coast. In one town, my father was a waiter, and my mother cleaned at a hotel. Then she became very ill."

He hung his head and stared at the dirt between his shoes. "She died two years ago because they waited too long to go to the hospital. It was too late by that time."

His words had a choked sound, and he stopped for a second.

"Why did they wait so long?" Nikki asked finally, her voice quiet.

"Because the hospital meant paperwork, and that meant a chance that they would find out about my parents being here illegally. We could not risk that. After she died, my father tried to honor what she wanted, to keep us here. There was never enough money, and the jobs never lasted. Finally, he began diving for sea urchins, and he taught me to dive with him. But the county began checking divers' permits, and we did not have one. Permits cost money—more money than we could ever get at one time."

"So what'd you do then?" Nikki asked.

Antonio sighed. "My father met Mr. Herrera-Ortiz." He sounded as though the taste of the name was bitter on his tongue. "He got my father work as a gardener at the university. It was supposed to be steady work, not like picking crops."

Nikki waited for a moment, turning back to the forgotten sewing in her lap, before she asked, "What happened?"

"What I told you. One day, my father did not come home. Two days later, Mr. Herrera-Ortiz, the man you saw

here yesterday, came and explained that my father had fled
. . . back to Mexico."

"Wait a minute," Nikki broke in. "Why would he do that?
And just leave you here?"

His answer was so low that Nikki had to bend her head
closer to catch his words. "Mr. Herrera-Ortiz said he was
caught smuggling—smuggling drugs. He ran away, rather
than be arrested."

A shiver ran through Nikki at the sound of his words. She
glanced at the sky overhead and the ocean in front of her and
saw that the fog was rolling in, thick and billowing, and the
sunlight had turned a leaden gray.

They sat for a while then in silence, and Nikki concen-
trated on doing the neatest sewing job she could. When she
was finally finished, Nikki knotted the red thread carefully on
the inside, snapped off the leftover, and held up the doll for
inspection to Mari, who had come back from the grove.

It would be a long time, Nikki thought, before she forgot
how Mari's black eyes shone at the sight of her fixed-up doll,
or the way her arms crept around Nikki's neck in a tight hug
of thanks.

Mari skipped off with the doll under her arm, and Nikki
and Antonio talked a little while longer. Finally, she glanced
down at her watch. "I'd better get going soon. I have to meet
my aunt for lunch, then work at the conference."

When Nikki started toward the hotel, her mind was
playing over and over the things Antonio had said. His stoic
acceptance of what had happened astonished her. As she
made her way back across the bluff and down the boulders, she
could still hear his voice describing what had happened when
Mr. Herrera-Ortiz told him about his father's leaving.

"I told him my father would never be involved in smuggling drugs—he *hated* drugs. He always warned me how much harm they could do to me. But Herrera-Ortiz only laughed and said life has many surprises. He said that he wanted to help us, that he would pay the rent if I worked for him, did odd jobs. And that he would bring us food. It is not enough, though, what he brings, and some days he forgets, so I fish. But some days, when I catch nothing, then I go to the hotel early, before many people come, to the breakfast." He had hesitated, then added defensively, "They throw most of that food away, you know. It is just wasted!"

"What kind of work are you doing for Mr. Herrera-Ortiz?" Nikki had asked.

Antonio had stared into the fog as though he could see through it. "Just odd jobs, small things he tells me to do when I meet him here." Again his voice had taken on that defensive tone. "And it is only for a short time. Until he helps my father get back."

Nikki had looked around at the ruined house and the boathouse. "But, Antonio, I don't understand. I mean, what could you do here that—" She broke off, staring at his bent head, at his hair, dark and thick, that fell forward over his forehead, and a chill ran down her back. She thought about all she'd heard about drug smuggling since coming to Santa Linnea, and suddenly, she *knew*. She began again, more slowly.

"What exactly is he making you do, Antonio?"

Antonio put his elbows on his knees and leaned his head into his hands. When he spoke, his voice was muffled. "He says it is only until I earn enough money to get my father back into the country. He knows a man, a guide, who brings people from Mexico by a way the border police do not know. Then we could move to another state, where they do not know what my father has done."

He had stood to his feet then and turned away from her, shutting her out, and she'd watched his shoulders stiffen under the T-shirt. "You don't understand. If it will help get my father back, then I have to do whatever they tell me to."

Nikki had looked at him, stunned. "I can't believe this!" she burst out. "You're going to just go ahead and do whatever they . . . They're trying to make you help smuggle drugs, too, aren't they?"

He had turned around to face her then, his dark eyes smoldering. "This is not your business," he said, his voice firm.

"Antonio, please!"

"No!" he'd answered angrily. "Now go away, Nikki. Leave us alone. Do not ask any more questions because this does not concern you."

She stepped off the last boulder onto the sandy beach, checked her watch, and began walking faster. "*This does not concern you,*" she heard his words again, like a door slamming shut in her face. *Don't I wish!* she thought. *It's like watching a crime show on TV. Except this is real.*

By the time she reached the hotel room, her mind was in a whirl. She shook her head as though to clear it, then opened the door and walked inside.

At the Beach Plum, Aunt Marta and Ted were already working their way through the appetizer basket of tortilla chips and salsa. Marta looked up as Nikki approached their table.

"Good morning, Nikki. We waited till you got here to order." She held out a menu to her niece, then regarded her more carefully. "Are you okay?"

It must show, Nikki thought. *I'll have to do better than this.* "Hi, Aunt Marta. *Reverend* Wilcox." Nikki grinned at him as she slid into her chair, and Ted responded by drawing himself up straighter and trying to look somber and dignified.

"If you're going to address me like that, then I have to act a whole lot more formal than I'm comfortable doing, especially on my day off." He turned to Marta. "I'm afraid that bringing her to hear me preach did my secret plan more harm than good."

Marta looked at him quizzically, one eyebrow raised in question. "Your *plan*, Ted? What are you talking about?"

"My plan to win over the heart of your favorite niece, in hopes of carving out a permanent place in her aunt's affections."

Marta raised both eyebrows and shook her head, then went back to scanning the menu.

Ted sighed and said with mock seriousness, "Oh, well, that's what I get for being devious."

But Nikki noticed as she watched him how intently he looked at Marta, as if he hoped she'd still raise her head and give a more satisfactory response.

Marta, though, seemed oblivious to Ted. Or at least that's what Nikki thought at first. Later on, after their salads were served, she began to sense another reaction in her aunt to Ted's words. *She's uneasy,* Nikki thought. *She's talking too fast, the way she does when she gets nervous, and she won't look at him.* It both amused and pained her to see her aunt, normally unflappable, show signs of self-consciousness.

Nikki poked at the green leaf lettuce and picked out squiggles of thinly sliced red cabbage from her salad as she listened to them talking. Ted seemed aware of Marta's uneasiness, and he steered the conversation to a more comfortable topic. They talked throughout lunch about the conference, which was due to open the next evening, Tuesday, and run through Sunday afternoon.

Finally, Marta folded her napkin loosely and laid it beside her plate. "Speaking of the conference," Marta said, "I need to get going. There are still a million details to take care of, including a seminar leader who was just taken to the hospital with appendicitis—that leaves four sessions uncovered. Come on, Nikki, I'll drop you off at MacKenzie's office."

Ted reached for the bill and asked, "I couldn't interest you two in a sunset sail, could I?"

It sounded wonderful to Nikki, but she didn't get to say so because, as the three of them got to their feet, she accidentally jarred the table. Ted's glass, still half full of Coke, wobbled dangerously. Nikki jumped back quickly, with an unpleasant vision of how MacKenzie would look at her if she arrived wearing splotches of soda down the front of her shirt. Ted's question got lost somehow in the laughing that followed.

"Watch out for her, Ted," Marta said. "It's Nikki's new strategy. She picks out the best-looking man around and douses him with soda—it's a whole new way of meeting guys."

❦ *Fourteen* ❧

WHEN MARTA DROPPED Nikki off at the university office, MacKenzie was nowhere in sight. Nikki poked her head into two of the other cubicles off the main workroom, but they were empty, too. *Everybody must still be at lunch,* she thought and dropped into a chair beside the floor-to-ceiling windows.

There were stacks and stacks of folders, already thick with papers, piled neatly on the long table by the copier, but Nikki had no idea what project she was to help with today, so all she could do was wait. She leaned back in her chair and watched the surfers bob like seals in the ocean in their sleek, black wetsuits. They clung to their surfboards, treading water, waiting for the next wave to break. To the left, on the bluffs above the beach, hang gliders and paragliders sailed effortlessly into the wind and out over the surfers like giant butterflies.

Nikki had been watching for several minutes when she gradually became aware of voices over the dim hum of the fluorescent lights. She could make out the sound of a low, bass voice speaking, then a lighter, higher voice answering, and both were coming closer to the workroom where she sat. Nikki swiveled in her chair and looked toward the hall that connected this wing of offices with the rest of the complex.

"And just how much longer do you think I can do this?" the higher voice was saying, taut and intense, as though it cost the speaker great effort to hang on to her self-control.

"Until the job is done, that's how long. That was our agreement, remember?" The voice sounded familiar to Nikki, and she had the feeling that she knew the man, even though his face was turned away from her. The loose beige cotton sports coat couldn't disguise his athletic build, but it wasn't until he reached up and tugged at his right earlobe that Nikki recognized the gesture and realized the man was Lee Tierney.

MacKenzie was the other speaker, and tall as she was, she had to look up at him as she answered. "We came within *inches* of being jailed yesterday, you know." Both her slender shoulders, tanned and flawless in her white sleeveless dress, and her chin were held high, but there was a look in her dark eyes that Nikki had not seen before. For once, it looked like someone other than MacKenzie was in control.

"And if you had, I'd have paid the bail. Just stay with me here—it's only for a few more weeks. You know that. Now look, MacKenzie, we need to get the plans going for the next demonstration. It's important for you to get the word out because you've got to keep in mind that the more people we can get there, the more impact it carries with the press."

"I know that, and I'll do it, but I still think *you* need to be there," she insisted. "*You* need to be involved."

"MacKenzie." His voice was warm and soothing as if he were dealing with a recalcitrant child. "You know perfectly well that's impossible. Once I was identified with this, my tenure here would be on the line, and if I lost my position, then where would the movement be? Hmmm?"

MacKenzie gave a delicate shrug and looked away.

Lee Tierney reached out and grasped her gently by the forearms. "Hey, what's happened to you, MacKenzie? You've always been the best supporter I've ever had! You're not going soft on me now, are you?"

MacKenzie looked back into his eyes for a second, then shook her head. "No, Lee. Of course not." There was just a hint of uncertainty in her voice.

"Well, that's a relief. If we want to preserve this coastline for the future, we *cannot* give up now. This is an extremely important cause we're fighting for, but the other side is always winning because people just get wrapped up in their own lives, they get too busy or whatever, and they drop out. This is the time to hang tough. Don't you see that? Someday, everybody who lives here will be thanking us." He slid his hands up and down her arms, encouraging her to see his point. MacKenzie nodded her head, and a small smile curved the corners of her mouth.

Nikki felt uneasy eavesdropping this way, though she had no idea what else she could have done. She cleared her throat lightly, and both MacKenzie and Dr. Tierney started and swung around to face her.

"Nikki! What are you doing here this early?" MacKenzie demanded, looking at her accusingly.

Nikki's first response was to answer her in kind, then she stopped and took a deep breath.

"Look, MacKenzie, all you told me was to come after lunch, remember?"

Dr. Tierney stepped forward and turned that wide, charming smile in Nikki's direction. "I'm sure she does. MacKenzie's very good at managing people."

Oh, right, Nikki thought. *If you count intimidation as a good management tool.*

He murmured something to MacKenzie that Nikki couldn't quite make out, then unfolded his sunglasses from the inside pocket of his jacket. "See you later, ladies." He smiled again at Nikki, kissed the air by MacKenzie's cheek, and strode toward the door to the parking lot. He turned the door handle, then stopped and looked back at MacKenzie. "Don't forget what I said," he told her, still smiling broadly, and Nikki had the feeling that all his geniality was especially for her benefit and meant to offset MacKenzie's obvious irritation.

MacKenzie turned and flounced off to her office without a word, and Nikki sighed, watching her go. *Seems like I'm destined to irritate MacKenzie no matter how hard I try to do otherwise,* she thought, smiling wryly.

When MacKenzie returned, she carried a thick stack of papers. She dropped them on the worktable closest to the copy machine and jabbed a long, pointed, perfectly manicured fingernail at the top page.

"We need 250 copies of this. It lists the name, address, and books or articles in print of everyone attending this conference. Each conferee has to get a copy. Then we have to put the last few information sheets into every orientation packet. But first, before you start on that, I'd better show you the housing for the conferees, so you can direct them tomorrow. Otherwise, you'll have to come running to me every time someone asks you for directions in the registration line. Some of them, like your aunt, choose to stay in hotels, but the majority stay here on campus. It's not far to the dorms, so we can walk."

There was so much tension in the air between them that Nikki felt she had to at least try to clear things up. "Look, MacKenzie," she said as they started for the door, "I had no idea that getting here early was going to be such a problem. I'm sorry if I interrupted something between you and Dr. Tierney—"

"Don't be ridiculous, Nikki. There is nothing between me and Dr. Tierney to interrupt," she said flatly. She reached up to her wraparound sunglasses, which acted as a kind of hairband, and slid them down into place. Nikki could no longer see her eyes.

"Are you in his biology class?" Nikki asked, making another attempt to smooth things over.

"Yes."

"He seems like a really great guy. Not to mention looking like a movie star."

"There's a lot more to Dr. Tierney than good looks, Nikki, and having a great personality. He's also one of the best professors in the whole university, and he's very involved in the community. He really cares about what goes on in this city, and he's not afraid to say so."

Nikki looked at MacKenzie, surprised to hear her say so much at one time, but there was more. "He fights for all kinds of environmental issues, because with his background as a biologist, he knows the risks of the oil companies drilling out in the channel and along the shore here. And he does other stuff, too—he even volunteers time to be a Big Brother and help kids in this community." MacKenzie spoke proudly, as though what Lee Tierney did reflected on her.

Nikki tried to keep the conversation going as they walked,

but MacKenzie quickly turned businesslike once again. She handed Nikki a copy of the map that would be given to all registrants and pointed out numbered dorms as they went.

"Towels and washcloths are changed daily. Other than that, people are on their own as far as housekeeping. You'll be giving out keys, so you need to know there's a five-dollar deposit on each one. What people ask about most are the times and locations for meals and meetings, so we put a schedule sheet right in the front of each packet. I just got the final information on Saturday night's banquet this morning, so I still have to type that up when we get back to the office. Then you can start assembling the packets."

When MacKenzie decided Nikki had seen enough of the campus to be able to direct registrants, they started back.

"We'll take the path along the cliffs to save time. It's a shortcut to the building where my office is."

MacKenzie's brisk pace and long strides left Nikki struggling to keep up. They crossed the wide grassy area where Nikki and her aunt had seen the demonstrators the first night they arrived on campus.

"This is so gorgeous," Nikki commented, gesturing with her hand to take in the lawn area and the view of the ocean beyond.

"Helton Common," MacKenzie said shortly. "It's named after one of the past professors. Students hang out here between classes, and sometimes, like when certain speakers come to campus, everybody comes here to listen."

Nikki could hear the surf crashing far below, but the beach was hidden from sight by the overhanging bluffs, even though she walked close to the edge and tried to see over. In two or three places, steps led up from the shore to the main path, and Nikki and MacKenzie passed several surfers, still clad in black wetsuits and carrying their boards, returning from the water. When Nikki turned to look back and take in the view of the coastline, she was surprised to see, not more than a mile away, what appeared to be the South Coast Inn. She stood still for a minute, trying to get her bearings.

"Look at that, MacKenzie." She pointed toward the hotel. "That's where we're staying, isn't it? It can't be more than a mile away. I had no idea it was this close."

"Well, naturally," MacKenzie answered, unimpressed. "That's because when you drive here, the road runs through town, and it's about three times as long. If you don't mind, I really need to get back to the office now."

Nikki nodded and took a few steps backward to show MacKenzie she was cooperating, but she couldn't tear her eyes away. If that was the hotel, then that bluff sticking out into the water—the farthest point she could see from here—was the place where she'd sat to watch the sunrise. And beyond it was the cove, completely hidden from view, where she'd discovered Mari and Antonio the day before.

She turned and jogged a few steps to catch up with MacKenzie. "So what's beyond that point?" she asked. "Farther up the coast?"

"Just some deserted coves and stuff," MacKenzie answered. "People used to live on the cliffs up there, but the land is very fragile. Every time we had a bad winter, a lot of houses got destroyed, so now it's just deserted." MacKenzie pushed her sunglasses back up as they entered the building, then spoke again. "A lot of us are taking advantage of the situation and trying to get that area declared off-limits as a seal rookery. It's one of Dr. Tierney's special projects."

Back in the office, MacKenzie started right in typing the schedule sheet. She was only halfway through when her phone rang. She listened silently, then began to protest. "But I'm right in the middle of typing. . . . You have to have it right now? You can't wait till . . . All right. I'll be there in a few minutes." She sighed and hung up, then turned to Nikki. "I really need to get this schedule done, but I have to run something over to the dean's office, so I guess you'll just have to wait till I get back."

Nikki looked at the schedule sheet on the computer screen. It was a simple matter of filling in the boxes with times and building names. She hesitated a second, then realized she was actually feeling satisfaction at seeing MacKenzie thrown into such confusion, and she was immediately ashamed of herself.

Lord, please forgive me, she prayed silently. *MacKenzie's not exactly my favorite person in the world, and I need help to really care about her. Help me know what You want me to do here.*

"MacKenzie, I can type. Why don't you just let me finish it for you?"

MacKenzie looked at Nikki, and for the first time, her expression softened. It was the closest thing Nikki had seen to a smile on her face.

"You wouldn't mind?" she asked. Then she added suspiciously, "You have to make sure it's absolutely accurate."

"No problem," Nikki said.

Ten minutes after MacKenzie left, Nikki finished the sheet. She proofread it quickly, then took it to the copy machine and started making copies. She worked steadily, her sense of accomplishment rising, as she inserted a bright yellow schedule in the front of each folder and doggedly kept her eyes off the surfers and paragliders outside. The office was quiet and pleasant, and she began to enjoy what she was doing. She'd always thought, growing up, that she would end up working at something related to music, the way her grandmother and mother and Aunt Marta all did, but that took years of college and graduate school. *Maybe secretarial work wouldn't be so bad,* she thought.

By the time MacKenzie walked back in the door, Nikki had finished stuffing all but the last dozen or so folders. MacKenzie picked up one of the extra yellow sheets and scanned it.

"Nikki!" she said, and her voice was sharp. "You didn't *proofread* this?"

Nikki straightened up and stared at her, a sinking feeling in the pit of her stomach. "Well, of course I did. Why? What's wrong?"

"You've transposed the numbers! The room where the A-track seminars are held is 213, not 321. Now people will go to the wrong floor, and everybody will get all confused and—" MacKenzie sighed and rolled her eyes and spoke in the direction of the ceiling. "I *knew* I should have done this myself. You know, the conference opens tomorrow. It's not like we have forever to get all this stuff done."

Nikki squirmed with embarrassment. How could she have made such a stupid mistake and not caught it?

"I'm sorry, MacKenzie. I *did* check it, but I was in a hurry to get it done for you and. . . ." Her voice trailed away as she watched MacKenzie walk back to her own office. Through the open doorway, Nikki could see her drop angrily into her chair beneath the huge green rain forest poster that read THE EARTH DOES NOT BELONG TO US. WE BELONG TO THE EARTH. MacKenzie leaned forward, maneuvering the mouse until her cursor was at the point of Nikki's error. With just a few quick, efficient keystrokes, she corrected it, then turned on the printer.

Nikki leaned against the worktable with her arms across her chest and hung her head. *How am I supposed to build a relationship with someone who can't stand the sight of me?*

❦ *Fifteen* ❦

BY THE TIME NIKKI FINISHED making 250 copies of the corrected schedule, removing the incorrect sheets, and inserting the new ones, the afternoon was half gone. She worked another hour, finishing the list of books and papers published by the attendees, then said good-bye to MacKenzie, who barely acknowledged her words.

"Registration starts at noon tomorrow," MacKenzie added as Nikki started to leave, "so you need to be here by 11:30 at the latest."

Nikki agreed, then hurried out the door to the parking lot, where Marta had said she'd leave the car. The sun was shining brilliantly on the blue water, and the ocean breeze blew gently across her face. The black interior of the Grand Am was hot, and she stood for a second with the door open, letting the cooler air flow in before she slid inside and started for the hotel.

The hotel room was clean and still, every trace of disorder she and Marta had made obliterated, and the heavy, sweet smell of air freshener hung over everything. Nikki tossed her purse on the bed and headed for the bathroom to get her bathing suit from the hook behind the door. There was nothing she wanted more than a quick dip in the sparkling water of the pool—maybe that would somehow wash away the ineptness that had so disgusted MacKenzie.

On the way to Santa Linnea, Nikki had been excited at the thought that she might even get a chance to tell MacKenzie about God. But now . . . *I think we can say I pretty much blew any chance of* that *happening!* Nikki thought as she wiggled into her suit. *MacKenzie thinks I'm an absolute idiot.*

And, although Nikki could hardly bring herself to admit it, even worse was the fact that MacKenzie's comments had stirred up doubts in her own mind. If someone as confident and intelligent as MacKenzie felt such scorn for Christianity, maybe Nikki should look at the whole thing a lot more closely. *What if it was all my imagination, or emotions, that day I thought I became a Christian?*

Marta had caught a ride back to the hotel with Alex so she and Nikki could have a quick dinner together before she returned to the university for the evening.

"I'll leave my laptop for you so you'll have something to do," she told Nikki as they sat in the restaurant. "I noticed when I was on-line today that you have a couple new E-mail messages you may want to answer. You can sign on without my help, can't you?"

Nikki nodded, then looked up as the waitress placed heaping dishes of fettuccine Alfredo in front of them.

Marta waited until she was out of earshot, then grinned and said, "You know what cardiologists call this stuff?"

Nikki shook her head, and Marta went on.

"Heart attack on a plate. It's nothing but butter and cream and eggs." She put a forkful in her mouth and chewed blissfully, her eyes shut. "Mmmm! This is worth a little risk, don't you think?"

Nikki forced a small laugh but said nothing.

"You're awfully quiet tonight, Nikki," Marta said, dabbing the napkin across her lips. "Did everything go all right with MacKenzie today?"

Nikki shrugged and explained her mistake with the schedule and MacKenzie's reaction to it.

They ate in silence for a minute, then Marta observed, "You know, I get the feeling there's more going on between you two than just a typo on the schedule."

Nikki twisted her fork around and around, concentrating completely on winding one long fettuccine noodle securely around the tines. When she finished, she spoke quietly. "Yeah. You're right." *Things aren't turning out anything like I expected. I thought that becoming a Christian meant . . . well, I'd be different. And life would work out better, somehow. If I even* am *a Christian, that is.*

"Well?"

"I don't even know how to explain it, Aunt Marta." She looked up. "Let's just say that I'm still doing a lot of thinking about Ted's sermon yesterday."

Marta didn't probe. They finished their dinner and, just as Nikki decided it was time to tell her aunt about Antonio and Mari, Marta said, "I really should get back to the university, and I'd like to take the car myself tonight so Alex doesn't have to bring me home again. Sure you wouldn't like to come with me so you won't have to stay here alone?"

Nikki shook her head. "No, thanks. It's been a long day. I may just lie around for a few hours and veg out in front of the TV."

"Okay, then. Would you mind if I just gave you one thing to think about before I go?"

Nikki shook her head.

"Sometimes faith can feel like a *very* risky business."

After Marta left, Nikki went back to the room. There were plenty of things she could do, but she found herself curling up in the blue chair, staring out the window at the cars on the road below. She prayed for Evan and for her grandparents back in Michigan, but somewhere in the middle of her prayer, her thoughts got sidetracked to what was going on right here in California.

She had tried and tried to figure everything out, make it all fit together. Instead, everything she'd gotten involved in seemed to end up a mess. MacKenzie not only didn't want to be friends, she didn't want anything to do with Nikki, and Nikki wasn't even sure why. And Antonio was really angry with her for butting in and would probably go right on with what he was doing and end up in jail, or worse, like his father. *I'm messing things up just like I always have, Lord,* she prayed silently. *So what do I do now?*

When the phone rang, she jumped and looked around to find that the room had turned completely dark. Unable to find the light switch, she stumbled hard against the sharp corner of the bedside table as she groped for the receiver in the dark.

"Ow!" she cried, grabbing at her leg and trying to compose her voice as she answered. "Hello!"

"Whoa. Is that you, Nikki?" a man's voice asked.

"Yeah, it's me," she answered, sinking down onto the bed and rubbing her shin.

"Well, this is Ted. Ted Wilcox. Are you all right? You sound upset."

Nikki laughed, embarrassed. "No, I'm . . . okay. The phone startled me is all, and I ran into some furniture in the dark. . . ." She trailed off, unwilling to say any more.

"What are you doing sitting there in the dark?" he asked. His voice held concern that felt oddly comforting to her.

"Just . . . thinking. About things," she answered.

There was silence for a minute. "Oh. Well, okay. Hey, is Marta around, by any chance?" There was such an obvious attempt to sound casual in his words that she felt immediately sorry for him.

"No, Ted, she's not. She said she wouldn't be back until late because she and Alex still have so much to do for tomorrow when the conference opens."

"Oh," he said again, disappointment evident in his voice. "Well, I'll try again another time then. You're sure everything's all right there, Nikki? Because, like I told you, if I can help you out with anything . . ."

"Thanks," Nikki said. "I really appreciate that." She meant to say good-bye then, but different words came out, words she hadn't planned. She listened to herself in surprise. "Actually, I need to ask you a question."

"Sure. What about?"

"Well, I probably need to ask you more than one. Do you have time?"

"Sure," Ted answered. "Why don't you meet me in the restaurant on the first floor?"

"Okay. How long will it take you to get here? Where are you right now?"

It was Ted's turn to sound embarrassed. "Well, actually, I'm right around the corner from your hotel. I can't exactly say it was just a coincidence either, so don't ask, okay? Let's just say I figured close proximity might work to my advantage if Marta was free tonight."

Nikki grinned, then struggled to keep from laughing out loud.

"So," he went on, "does that suit you? Meeting at the restaurant, I mean?"

"That's fine," she answered. "I'll be right down."

At first, their talk skirted the real questions whirling around in Nikki's head. Ted told her how it felt to live on board the *Wind Dancer* and enthused about the freedom of not being tied to a run-of-the-mill house and yard.

"I know I won't always be able to live like this," he said, "but right now, it's great to be able to sail whenever I want. The best place I know to pray and plan and do my heavy thinking is out in the bay beneath a full moon, just listening to the water slosh against the sides of the boat and the seals barking from those big buoys they crawl up on. You should see it then, Nikki. You can actually read on deck sometimes, it's so bright, and the moonlight on the water—" he shook his head and smiled at her "—that's something I can't put into words. You just have to see it for yourself."

"How'd you come up with such a neat name for the sloop?" Nikki asked.

Ted smiled. "That was easy. It's a kind of metaphor for my

own life, when I'm really listening to what God is telling me. Just like the sloop responds to the wind, to the changes in direction and such, that's how I want to respond to the Spirit of God, wherever He directs me." He spoke so easily, so unself-consciously, that Nikki felt a pang of longing, listening to him.

How does somebody get that kind of confidence in God? she wondered, spooning up the last of her ice-cream sundae. *I mean, here I am, at least some of the time, trying to figure out if God's even there, and Ted talks like he knows Him so well that all he has to do is listen and he hears Him talking!* She was dying to ask more questions but felt too self-conscious. Instead, she turned the conversation to her questions about immigration and illegal aliens.

By the time he finished his own ice cream, Ted was starting to understand that Nikki's interest was more than just academic. He set his spoon down and leaned forward across the table.

"Nikki, what's making you ask all these questions?"

Nikki swallowed hard. Now she'd done it. The last thing Antonio wanted was for someone else to know what was going on. *He'd be a lot happier if I'd never even found out.*

On the other hand, she hadn't *promised* not to say anything, and she couldn't just pretend she didn't know. How could she do nothing, when they might very well be in some kind of danger? She pictured Herrera-Ortiz's broad smile as he ripped the dress on Mari's doll.

"Um, I really can't say a lot. Just that I met somebody— two somebodies, actually—who're here illegally. And I think they may be in some kind of danger."

Ted's eyes narrowed. "Wait a minute. How old are these

'somebodies'? I can tell you this makes me worried—people involved in this kind of stuff can be dangerous."

Nikki couldn't help but hear the deep concern in his voice. "I hear you, Ted, I hear you. But I don't think there's any danger in this situation." She tried to ignore the voice in her head saying, *Oh, sure! With Herrera-Ortiz?*

"Just know I'm uneasy with this. How'd you meet these two? And are they adults or what?"

"Couldn't you just give me information for right now?" Nikki countered.

"Well, I guess so," Ted said reluctantly. "What's the question?"

"What can you tell me about the guides that bring people over the border illegally? I mean, do people really do that for money?"

"Oh, all the time, Nikki," he answered. "It's a big business. Usually, we're not even aware it's going on, but every so often there's an accident, or they get caught, and then there's a write-up in the paper. Last month, for instance, there was a truck that came over the border down near Jacumba—naturally, they pick deserted, out-of-the-way places to cross—crammed with two dozen men. The Border Patrol started following them, and the truck sped up to get away." He shook his head sadly, running his index finger absently around the rim of his bowl. "Eight men were killed and 15 injured. They never found the other one. And you can bet each one of those men paid a good price to get to that kind of 'freedom.' "

He paused for a moment, then went on. "Last year, the big concern was fires. The guides would bring their people in by foot over some very desolate mountain country, where it got really cold at night. They'd start fires to keep warm, the fires would spark into dry grass or get blown by the wind, and the next thing you knew, a whole hillside was burning out of control."

"What happens when these people get caught?"

"The INS sends them back, and that's the end of it. Unless they've gotten into trouble while they were on this side of the border, of course."

Nikki laid down her napkin and propped her chin with one hand. "Wait a minute. I need to know more about that. Like, what if somebody was here illegally and got caught smuggling drugs?"

"*That* would be a whole different story. If convicted, they'd serve their time, then be deported. And they probably aren't ever going to get the chance to come back here again, unless they can slip in unnoticed, that is. Drug smuggling is such a big problem here, partly because it's an incredibly easy way to get rich that people are willing to take the risk involved. So the laws to stop it are very tough. All an illegal needs is just the *rumor* of being involved, and he's in big trouble."

Ted laid both hands flat on the tabletop, his fingers spread slightly. His bushy eyebrows were low over his eyes, and he looked at her intently. "All right, Nikki. It's time to talk turkey. Illegal immigration is one thing. Drug smuggling is something totally different."

Nikki looked at him uneasily. "I shouldn't say any more tonight. Give me another day or two, okay? Then I will. But in the meantime, can you just answer one more question?"

Ted nodded. "Nikki—"

"No, no, this is an easy question. Would you and the people at your church be willing to help if I could talk this person into coming to you?"

"Absolutely," Ted said. "I mean, if there's any way we can, then we have to. That's part of what our Christianity is all about."

"Good. That's what I needed to hear. And don't worry, I'll be really careful. I'm not into danger and adventure and all that kind of stuff."

He laughed then, and the tension was broken. "I guess you're not as much like Marta as I thought, huh?"

As they left the restaurant, they passed the hotel gift shop where a display that included some good-looking ties caught Nikki's eye. She stopped suddenly. "Ted? Would you come in here with me for just a minute?"

Ted stopped, looking at her questioningly. "Why? You need something?"

Nikki laughed and led him inside. "No, Ted. *You* need something."

"What?"

"Just come on."

They went inside, and Nikki steered him to the display. "Don't you think these ties are really nice?"

Ted shrugged. "Yeah. They're okay. You know, I'm not really much into clothes—" He stopped, and she could see realization dawning in his eyes. "Oh. You mean, one of these ties might be better than, say, what I wore in church yesterday?"

Nikki grinned at him. "Well, let's just say that I know what Aunt Marta likes. Stick with me, and I'll give you good advice. I recommend the blue one."

Ted rolled his eyes in mock exasperation, but all the same, he took the blue tie to the counter and pulled out his wallet, then turned and said under his voice, "Nikki! Did you see the price tag on this thing?"

"Trust me, Ted. It's worth it."

Back in the room, Nikki plugged in Marta's laptop and looked up her E-mail. She found a message from Carly that made her laugh.

Nikki!

WHY HAVEN'T YOU WRITTEN??!! Oops—my all-knowing brother, otherwise known as the great electronics guru, just informed me that capitals on the Internet are "just like shouting and considered very bad manners." (Of course, you'll notice he didn't say what reading over someone else's shoulder is considered!) Anyway, pardon my bad manners.

So how's it going? I figure the reason we haven't heard from you is that you've met some absolutely gorgeous guy who's taking up all your time, and you're sitting around the pool with him, and taking sunset walks on the beach and all the rest of that Southern California stuff. Am I on the right track? Close? Nearly clairvoyant, huh? So I know you just don't have time to waste at the keyboard.

But, like I told you, I understand. Remember that guy next door I told you about? I'm pretty busy myself, just watching him. Well, write SOON. (Oops, sorry, did it again.)

P.S.—Jeff says hi and he'll write later—he has a big exam tomorrow.

Nikki put her fingers on the keys and stared at them for a minute, then began.

Hey, Carly!

Sorry I haven't written. I did meet a guy, and we did walk on the beach, but it's a little different from what you're thinking. . . .

Nikki closed her eyes and shook her head. *Boy, is it ever!* she thought. *In fact, that may be the understatement of the year.*

❧ *Sixteen* ❧

BY MIDMORNING ON TUESDAY, Nikki was jogging through the soft morning fog toward the boathouse, excitement growing inside her as she thought about the help she now had to offer Antonio and Mari. *This is so neat, Lord,* she prayed as she ran. *I guess this is more the way I expected things to work out after I believed in You. I can't wait to tell Antonio.*

Mari was playing outside, squatting in the dusty grass in front of the boathouse door, lining up white pebbles in a circle on the cement step. The doll was clenched unceremoniously against her side, under one arm, so that both of her small hands were free. She was chanting the same tune about the *mariposa* in her high, quavery singsong, totally absorbed in what she was doing.

"Mari," Nikki called from behind her.

The girl's thin little body straightened out and whirled around. When she saw who it was, Mari smiled her shy smile and looked eagerly at both of Nikki's pockets. Nikki realized with a pang that she was hoping for some food.

Just you wait, Mari, she thought. *Wait till the people at Ted's church see you. They're gonna love you, and I don't think food will be any problem at all.*

Nikki heard the same muffled dragging sounds from inside the boathouse as she had the day before, then the door creaked open, and Antonio looked around it. "Mari? You okay—" He stopped when he saw Nikki standing there, then stepped outside and shut the door quickly behind him.

"I can only stay a few minutes," Nikki began. "I'm supposed to work registration at the conference all afternoon. But I wanted to come and tell you some good news."

Antonio stuffed both hands into the pockets of his jeans and waited, his dark eyes watching her silently.

"See, I thought a lot about the things you said, and about what that man said and the way he threatened you. And I know you said you didn't need help. . . ." Nikki could feel herself sputtering under the intensity of those eyes. She realized that Antonio looked less than happy—*a lot* less—and she suddenly wondered why she'd thought this was such a great idea. She tried to keep going. "And I know this guy—a pastor— whose church helps immigrants. You know, people like . . ."

By now, Antonio's eyes were glaring. "Like us? Is that what you mean? And so you *told him?*" He blew out a mouthful of air through tight lips, then turned and kicked a stone with all his might. The stone skittered across the sandy ground and disappeared over the cliff toward the ocean.

Nikki tried to squelch what was running through her mind as she watched him. *He's even better looking when he's mad.*

For a minute, there was no sound besides the noise of the surf crashing on the beach far below. Antonio turned and took a step toward her, and Nikki cowered back.

"You *told!* And I trusted you. You came here where you should not have come, and you listened to things you should not have heard, and then you went and told—"

"Antonio, you're not listening to me. This church has helped a lot of people, and they're willing to help you!" It was Nikki's turn to be angry—angry that Antonio was being so bullheaded, that he wouldn't even consider Ted's offer of help, but most of all, that once again, things weren't turning out the way she'd thought they would. Frustration drove her to speak much more sharply than she should have. "Now, look! I had no intention of eavesdropping when I came here before. I'm sorry I heard what that man said to you. I'm sorry I turned up here at the wrong time. I'm sorry, you hear me? But I can't change what happened, and I can't change what I heard. And I happen to think you're in a lot of trouble."

Antonio stared at her, speechless, and she went on, even over the nagging little voice that sounded a warning in her head.

"I know that guy with the mustache is trying to get you involved somehow in something illegal, like drugs." She stopped short for a second, surprising even herself, but she could see from his face that she'd hit a nerve. "And you can't do that. You can't put yourself in danger that way. What if you get arrested? What will happen to Mari?"

He closed his eyes tightly, as if he were trying to shut out the sound of her words.

Nikki wanted so desperately for him to understand what she was saying, to agree with her, that she kept going. "Antonio, getting involved in drug smuggling is *wrong*— wrong for all the people those drugs will hurt. And it's dangerous for Mari and for you."

His chin came up then, like a fighter's. "If my father could do it, I can, too."

That was the last straw. He just wasn't thinking, that was all. What she was saying made perfect sense. Anybody could see that. He couldn't miss the sense of it unless he was *trying* to. Nikki clamped her hands to her hips angrily. "So are you saying you don't *want* help, Antonio? That you won't take it?"

Antonio looked very tired suddenly. When he spoke, his voice was flat and emotionless.

"This is not your business, Nikki. Go away now. Go and leave us alone."

He called Mari and led her by the hand into the boathouse, then closed the door firmly behind them.

A casual observer could never have told that MacKenzie was still upset by Nikki's mistake of the day before. But Nikki could.

There was something humiliating about the way MacKenzie overexplained every single thing she told Nikki to do as they set up the registration line, speaking just a little more slowly and distinctly than she needed to. By the time MacKenzie showed her where to file the registration forms conferees would be filling out and emphasized for at least the third time how essential it was that she make sure the forms were filled out *completely*, Nikki was squirming inside at being treated as though she were unusually slow.

And all because of one typo! This girl doesn't cut anybody any slack, that's for sure.

She thought of a million comebacks to let MacKenzie know how upset she was getting, then thought better of each one. It was as though a small voice was inside her head these days, telling her to restrain the same temper she would have unleashed just a few weeks ago.

Registration opened at noon, and Nikki and MacKenzie sat side by side behind a long, wood-grained table set up in the stuffy athletic center, where the air smelled faintly of sweat socks. They doled out registration forms and name tags and folders of material, including the corrected yellow schedule, to a seemingly endless line of registrants.

After the first hour or so, the job became so routine that Nikki's mind began skipping back to Mari and Antonio. She kept trying to push the thoughts of them away, but it was like throwing a boomerang. How had everything gone so wrong with Antonio, anyway? She'd been so sure she was helping, but now she'd made everything a million times worse.

She handed a name tag and folder to a tall, thin man with a head of busy, graying curls that hung nearly to his shoulders.

I was just trying to make Antonio see that drug smuggling is nothing to mess around with, she justified herself.

Behind the man, two middle-aged women reached for their folders, and Nikki turned on a polite smile as she gave them their materials. But inside, her mind was racing.

How was I supposed to know he'd get so upset? Her first response was to get angry and blame it all on him. *If he had any brains at all, he would have listened to me—* But that voice in her head refused to let her off the hook. It said that she could have been far more tactful, a lot wiser.

There was a lull in the line. She and MacKenzie had been sitting there, unoccupied, for three or four minutes when one of the students working at the table beside theirs took advantage of the quiet and turned in their direction.

"So, MacKenzie, you ready for Friday night? Should be another good party. Course that last one wasn't half bad, if you don't count the police, that is—"

MacKenzie frowned at him and shook her head back and forth, almost imperceptibly, glancing back toward Nikki.

Nikki tried to pretend she didn't notice, but she could see him lean out around MacKenzie to get a good look at her, the cause of his being hushed.

"So bring her along," he said, then began to talk to Nikki directly. "Hey, you'd like to come to our party, wouldn't you?"

"Jeremy, would you *please* stop it," MacKenzie broke in.

"O-*kay*," he said, drawing out the syllables as he thought of another topic. "So, did you hear the news about the drug bust in town this past weekend? Down there on Cortez Street—you know that little Mexican place where we all went for quesadillas that one night? It was right around the corner from there. I guess it was quite the big deal."

"Quite the big waste of time, you mean," MacKenzie shot back. "All that time and money and hassle over one little patch of marijuana growing in some guy's backyard. Now *there's* an efficient use of taxpayer money for you."

"Oh, I get it," Jeremy said. "This is where you start spouting Tierney's stuff about making drugs legal and all that, right? You swallow everything he says, don't you?"

MacKenzie gave a small sniff. "You know as well as I do that marijuana is very safe. It's natural, it comes right from the earth, and we respect that. It's only the authority types who try to keep people from using it because they can't stand to see anybody having a good time."

"Now there's a quote that sounds like it comes directly from a certain biology professor I know. Could it be the same one who does a whole lecture on how authority was made to be questioned? When'd you turn into such a Tierney groupie, MacKenzie?"

MacKenzie looked down at the table in front of her, and Nikki heard her answer in a low, furious voice. "Don't ever call me that again, do you hear? And don't waste your time trashing Tierney. If just half the professors on this campus were as decent as he is, this would be a lot better place to go to school." She jerked her head back up, and her sleek russet hair swung immediately back into place. "Besides, if you're so dead set against Dr. Tierney, why are you always at his parties?"

Jeremy leaned back in his chair, hands behind his head. "Let's just say I like the refreshments he provides." He laughed easily, unaffected by MacKenzie's anger, then leaned forward again to look around her at Nikki. "So why don't you plan on being here Friday night? You'd have a great time, I can promise you that. Everything gets going about 8:00, over at Helton Common. There're a couple bands coming—one from L.A. and some of our local guys who are pretty good."

Two more conferees came to the table, and everybody settled back to work.

In the next lull, Nikki asked the question she'd been mulling over for the last few moments. "MacKenzie? Are you really in favor of making drugs legal?"

MacKenzie looked at her as if she'd asked a question that had a perfectly obvious answer. "Yes, I am."

"But how can you feel that way?" Nikki asked, thinking of some of the kids she'd known at school who started smoking marijuana and gradually lost interest in everything besides the drug.

MacKenzie gave a long sigh and set down the money she

was counting. "Look, Nikki, our opinions are light-years apart. You know why? Because that's what *you* and *I* are—light-years apart."

Nikki started to shake her head to disagree, but MacKenzie went on. "My mother went on and on about you when your aunt called and said you were coming. I know all about what a great pianist you are and how your grades are perfect and that you're a Christian, which is not something that normally impresses her, but I think she figures all that good morality stuff might just rub off on me if she forces me to spend enough time with you. Why do you think she got you for this job, anyway? She could have hired a temp anywhere." She picked up the bills she'd set down and resumed her counting.

It was the longest single speech Nikki had ever heard MacKenzie make, and she sat perfectly still, stunned at first. Yet now there was a feeling inside that all the missing puzzle pieces about MacKenzie were finally fitting themselves into the empty spaces.

So that's why she couldn't stand me, right from the beginning. Here all this time I thought she was looking at me and thinking how clumsy and unsophisticated I was, and it was all because her mother forced . . . all because she thought I was some kind of great . . .

Nikki shook her head to clear the fog.

Oh, brother. If only you knew the real story, MacKenzie. That I've possibly been the most mixed-up person on earth this past year, with the pregnancy and everything else that happened. But somehow, you missed that part!

How could MacKenzie help it? The small, quiet voice in her head was back. *In your pride,* it said, *you've done everything you could to hide what really happened. Instead of caring enough about*

MacKenzie to tell her the truth, you were only concerned that you came across looking good.

MacKenzie's slim fingers slid the bills rapidly from one hand to the other, her full lips moving slightly as she murmured the numbers to herself.

"MacKenzie, there're a few things I think maybe you should know," Nikki began, but MacKenzie gave her head an impatient shake to stop her and went on counting. When she finally put the stack of bills into the cash box, she looked up at Nikki.

"What is it you think I have to know?"

"Well, just that . . . that . . . well, there's a whole lot more to the story than what you've heard. About me becoming a Christian and all."

"Really." MacKenzie's voice was a statement, not a question. "Look, Nikki, I don't think you understand what I'm saying. I'm not into conversion stories. I'm not into religion at *all*. I got way beyond that years ago when I started to understand that it grew out of a very primitive, crude stage of human development. I mean, look at the kind of people religion has produced and you'll see my point. I have no desire to be narrow-minded and prejudiced and spend my life trying to force everyone else into a certain mold. I want to be someone who makes a difference in the world, like . . . like Dr. Tierney."

She was interrupted as Jeremy leaned forward again. "Hey, so are you gonna be there, both of you? Friday night?"

MacKenzie answered before Nikki could say a word, and her voice was sharp-edged with sarcasm. "I'm sure this is not Nikki's type of party."

"Well, you're wrong, MacKenzie!" Nikki shot back. "You don't really know anything about me, and yes—" she directed her words to Jeremy "—I'd love to come."

"Hey, all right!" Jeremy responded. "I'll see you there."

Another group of conferees walked in the door, and Nikki ran through the routine with a smile she hoped masked her frustration. How was she ever supposed to make any kind of progress with MacKenzie when she had all these impossible strikes against her before she ever got started? *Not that I've helped matters much since I've been here, with all my fumbling.*

Just last night, Ted had talked about responding to God like his sloop responded to the wind, and it had sounded so good to her. But somehow she didn't think this was exactly what he'd had in mind. Jeff and Carly and Marta and her grandparents—they were always talking about God leading them and directing their path and stuff.

So how come it's not working for me? she wondered. *You know, God, I was so sure things would be different after I trusted You, but everything I touch here seems to fall apart. I seem to be doing a lot more harm than good, so I'm officially giving up on both MacKenzie and Antonio.*

❧ *Seventeen* ❧

WEDNESDAY MORNING, Nikki got up with plans to split her day between sight-seeing and cultivating her tan by the hotel pool. The idea was to keep so busy that she would finally quit thinking about MacKenzie and Antonio.

The plan worked well for the first half hour, but then the phone rang as she was getting ready. It was MacKenzie. Somewhere along the way, her voice seemed to have lost its critical overtones. She actually managed to sound sincere.

"Listen, Nikki, I hate to impose on you after the long day we had yesterday and everything, but we have a little problem over here. One of the conference speakers was going through his notes at the last minute—he's supposed to speak this afternoon—and he found out his secretary back in Kansas left out a whole page of sources in his bibliography. He could get into a lot of trouble, quoting people and not citing them, and he happens to be a really good friend of my mother's, so she brought him to me."

Nikki gave a noncommittal "uh-huh," so MacKenzie continued.

"*My* problem is that I promised Lee—" she caught herself "—Dr. Tierney that I'd go with him on a field project this morning. The results of this study he's been doing for the last month have to be recorded today, and he can't do it alone. So I was wondering if you might, perhaps, be available to help out just one more time." She went on hurriedly. "I know this is supposed to be your vacation, but then I thought, *Well, she's probably getting bored by now anyway with nothing to do but sit by the pool.*"

Nikki put the mascara wand back into the container. *You always think you know what's going on in my mind, don't you? And you're usually wrong.*

While she hesitated, MacKenzie spoke again. "He says he'll pay you double what the conference was paying. It's that important to him, Nikki."

The least she could do was show MacKenzie she was willing to act like a friend, even if the favor wasn't returned. "All right. I'll be there in a few minutes," she said.

By the time the missing page was typed and the copier broke down not once but twice, Nikki watched the clock hands move all the way to 12:55 before she could rush the completed papers to the auditorium where the anxious speaker was due to begin his presentation in five minutes.

Marta caught up with her in the back of the building after the papers were delivered. "Nik, what are you doing here? I thought your work was all done once registration was over."

Nikki told her about MacKenzie's phone call.

"Well, that explains it," Marta said. "I've been trying to call you all morning. I talked to Ted earlier—" she raised both eyebrows and talked on, trying not to acknowledge Nikki's exaggerated smile "—and this is the perfect day to go out on his boat."

"How can you get away from the conference that long?" Nikki asked over the sound of clapping from the auditorium behind them as the speaker was introduced.

"My work's basically done," Marta answered. "The hard part was getting everything in place, but now things should move along with just an occasional nudge from Alex and me. Besides, there's free time every afternoon to give everybody a chance to go sight-seeing or whatever. That's part of the reason we hold the conference here in Santa Linnea." She checked her watch and said, "Anyway, we're supposed to meet Ted at 2:30 down on the dock. You'll love it, Nikki— every year we manage to get out at least once and it is so—"

Nikki put her hands on her hips. "Aunt Marta, are you telling me you and Ted go sailing together every year when we all think you're out here *working*?" She grinned wickedly and leaned closer to her aunt. "Now let me just make sure I've got this straight. This *is* the same Ted you say is only a friend, right?"

Marta rolled her eyes toward the ceiling and muttered, "Give me a break!" Then she looked back at Nikki. "Just for that, you get to play errand girl." She gave her niece instructions about what clothes and shoes she needed from the hotel, and reminded her to bring jackets for both of them.

Nikki leaned back against the white seat cushions of Ted's sloop, her legs stretched out in front of her, ankles crossed, in the pleasant warmth of the afternoon sun. The sea breeze blew gently against her face and lifted tendrils of her hair with light fingers of air. It was only a 10-minute drive from the university campus to the harbor where the *Wind Dancer* sat rocking gently in the water, but once Nikki and Marta were on board and the boat got under way, she felt as if they were in a whole different world.

Marta was perched high in the opposite corner of the sloop on a seat that had been bolted in place over the stanchions like a small platform. She curled her feet around metal supports beneath her and looked down at Nikki and smiled. "It's great, isn't it?"

Nikki nodded, smiling back, and watched as Ted turned the wheel expertly, then let it glide back part way through his hands as he maneuvered his way around a long sandbar packed with gulls and pelicans. They reached the end of the channel, and Nikki watched with delight as they passed close by the huge red buoy, where a dozen or more seals basked in the sun. One seal lifted his snout into the air and barked loudly, then slid off into the water. The buoy rocked violently for a minute, its bell clanging, but the other seals lay still, undisturbed by all the commotion.

When they started for open water, Ted motioned to Marta, and she slid down from her seat and took the wheel so he could make his way forward to unfurl the sails. His motions were surefooted, careful but confident, in rubber-soled deck shoes, and he unsnapped the navy-blue sail covers and unfurled the jib with quick fingers.

Nikki turned back to see the harbor, which looked like a postcard scene with its yachts and fishing boats and the white sails dotting the bay around them. Then she gazed up at the beautiful houses that climbed the steep hills beyond. She found herself wondering where in this kind of world there could be a place for people like Antonio and Mari. *Leave it alone already, Nik!* she told herself angrily. *Antonio doesn't want your help, remember?*

She forced herself to watch Ted again to get her mind off them. He hauled on lines and adjusted things Nikki didn't understand and soon had both sails up all the way. They caught the wind and billowed out above the sloop.

Then came a moment Nikki thought she would never forget. Marta cut the motor at a signal from Ted, and silence enveloped them. Without the motor throbbing, the sloop seemed to skim across the water effortlessly.

Ted motioned Nikki to come forward, and she went slowly, placing each foot with care, till she stood even with him. He patted the hull beside him.

"You have to sit out here, at least for a few minutes, Nikki. It's required for all new sailors."

"What about Marta?" she asked as she crouched down beside him.

"Don't worry about your aunt—she does a pretty fair captain imitation, especially on a calm day like this. So what do you think?"

Nikki stared at the water rushing under the prow of the boat. If she looked straight ahead, toward the islands, there seemed to be nothing between her and the water, and the speed and smoothness were exhilarating. She glanced at Ted and said, "I think it's great. Thanks for bringing me."

"No problem," he said, smiling. "I happen to think everybody should sail, but then, I'm a little biased." His voice turned serious then. "Nikki, is there any update on what we talked about last night? The people you wanted our church to help?"

She gave a halfhearted shrug. "Not really, Ted. I guess I may just keep out of the whole thing." *Not like I have much choice.*

Ted couldn't hide the look of relief on his face. "That's good to hear. I have to confess, I thought a lot today about what you told me, and I got more and more concerned. You could've gotten yourself into a real mess if you got involved in this." He stood up and reached a hand out to help her do the same. "Let's get back to Marta, okay?"

Marta wasn't ready to give up the wheel yet, so Ted and Nikki sprawled comfortably on the padded seats, and Ted told her about the sailing races he entered on weekends and described his five-day trip the past autumn to Cabo San Lucas. He laced his hands behind his head and leaned back.

"Best fishing in the entire world is right there in Cabo, Nik. I brought in six mahimahi in one day."

He held his arms apart to illustrate the size of the fish, and Nikki asked, "And what'd you do with six of them in one day?"

"Oh, there's this guy on the beach down there who cleans and fillets them for you, then sells whatever you don't want to the restaurant. They grilled one for me." He shook his head back and forth slowly, obviously savoring the memory. The wind blew suddenly stronger against Nikki's face, and Ted turned and pointed his thumb to the left, smiling back at Marta. "This is the life," he said, "soaking up the sun while you do all the work, Marta. Maybe you'd like to come along more often?"

Marta smiled back briefly but didn't reply.

Nikki felt the boat change course slightly beneath her and

realized they were once again headed straight toward the islands, though she hadn't even noticed that they had drifted. She watched Marta's movements with interest. "How do you know how to steer?" she asked. "I mean, it's not like a car, where there are wheels underneath."

Ted sat forward. "Well, when she turns the wheel, it moves the rudder underneath. See, you have this combination of forces going on, between the wind that fills the sails, the water, which exerts a lot of force the boat has to work against, and the—"

Marta broke in, laughing. "I turn the wheel, Nik."

Ted flashed her a mock-exasperated look and then laughed with her. "Okay, okay. So you don't want to hear my whole technical speech on this. It's your loss." He got to his feet. "Come on, Nikki. You take a turn at being captain, and you'll understand better."

Nikki got behind the wheel. Marta shivered a little in the cool breeze and headed for the cabin.

"I think I'll get a cup of tea. Want some?"

They both nodded, then Nikki went back to listening to Ted's words. "You tell which way the wind is blowing from the telltale, but the—"

"Wait," Nikki said, "what's a telltale?"

In answer, Ted pointed at the piece of red string tied to the mast. "See how it blows? It'll tell you which way the wind is blowing. But the most important thing is to set your course by something that doesn't move—like the islands. Then, as you steer, you can keep making course adjustments as you need to. Like this." He turned the boat back toward the mainland. "Actually, that's not bad advice for life, either—setting your course by something that doesn't move. That's why it's so important to spend time in the Bible every day." He laughed at himself good-naturedly. "I think I feel a great sermon illustration coming on, but I guess I'll save it for Sunday."

She took the wheel alone and, after a few minutes, said, "You know what? This is no harder than driving a car."

"It's not rocket science. All you have to do is put yourself in the right position to catch the wind, then be ready to move when it blows."

When Nikki became comfortable enough steering the boat to glance around at the scenery, she was surprised to see how far west they had come.

"Look! That's the university, on the bluffs there, isn't it?"

Ted nodded. "Yes, it is. And off to the left is your hotel. Right there—see it?"

She looked in the direction of his outstretched arm and nodded. Then she scanned the beach where she jogged and the bluff where she had watched the sunrise that first morning. From this vantage point, Nikki could see right around it and into the cove where she'd met Antonio and Mari. She stared at the edge of the cliff, where the boathouse sat among the eucalyptus trees, searching for any evidence of Antonio and Mari being there, any movement, but the boat was too far out.

"Ted, can we get a little closer?" she asked. "So we could see into that little cove?"

Ted followed the direction of her gaze, then frowned. "That one? That's called Seal Cove. There used to be a beautiful house standing right on the edge of the cliff. But we had the most terrible winter—at least, terrible for this part of the country. Between the rains and the high surf, a huge section of the bluffs crashed right down into the water, and the house came with it, of course. There is a huge insurance case being argued about that land in the courts here. And the insurance companies have had enough. They're finally starting to say, 'Hey, you want to live in such a dangerous place? Fine, but you'll have to do it without our insurance.' So now there's nobody there but the seals."

I wouldn't count on it, Nikki thought, but Ted was still talking.

"And since no one ever goes there anymore, the seals have started using it as a breeding ground. In fact, I hear Lee Tierney is waging quite a battle to have it declared off-limits to people so the seals won't be disturbed, and he has most of the environmental people on his side."

"So can we get closer?" Nikki asked again.

"Well, sure, but why are you so interested in Seal Cove?" Ted asked, helping her turn the wheel so that *Wind Dancer* headed gradually toward the cove. "I mean, if it's seals you want to see, you'll get a better view back in the harbor, where they hang out on the buoys."

"Uh, it's not exactly the seals," she said, and Ted didn't probe any further.

But when they got nearer, Nikki was disappointed. This closer view showed little more than what she'd been able to see from farther out. Just a small dock—the kind you'd expect where there had been homes before and steps leading up the steep bluff to the boathouse.

Nikki flexed her fingers to relax them, then curved them around the metal wheel again and felt the movement of the boat beneath her hands as the wind picked up.

She grinned at Ted. "I could learn to like this. A lot."

He smiled back at her. "Remember what I told you? About why I named her the *Wind Dancer*? In the Bible, the wind is a symbol for the Holy Spirit."

Without realizing it, Nikki made a face, and Ted raised his eyebrows, waiting.

"I guess I must not know how to put my sails up yet, Ted, because I sure don't seem to be making any progress. In being a Christian, I mean."

"How's that?" he asked.

"The people I know who are Christians—like the Allens, our friends back in Chicago—and Aunt Marta and my grandparents, they all seem to have these great, successful spiritual lives, you know? They talk about how God leads them and answers their prayers and, well, it just doesn't work for me. Maybe there's something really wrong with me."

Ted listened quietly, waiting to make sure she was finished before he commented. "I don't think that's the problem, Nikki. I wonder if, just maybe, you're trying to get the plan for your own Christian life from watching other people. Some of that's all right, but sooner or later you're going to find out that God doesn't do the one-size-fits-all thing. He has a unique, tailor-made plan for each of us. Our responsibility is to spend enough time alone with Him, get to know Him so well, that we can hear what that plan is."

❦ *Eighteen* ❦

NIKKI PLANNED TO TAKE Thursday morning nice and slow, sleeping in till 9:00, jogging on the beach—in the opposite direction from Seal Cove—and then sight-seeing and taking herself to lunch on the wharf. She wouldn't waste a single minute thinking about Antonio and all that had happened with him, either.

While she wandered in and out of the little shops on the wharf, though, she realized she was not so much upset at Antonio as she was at herself. *He doesn't want my help? Fine! Let him figure out his problems on his own,* she thought. But she could feel the stirrings of anger curling around inside her, and she couldn't get rid of the guilt she felt each time she saw a child who looked Mari's age. And there were lots of them playing on the beach and at the playgrounds she passed and walking the streets with their parents.

A sense of futility seemed to hang over everything she'd tried to do, at least since she'd become a Christian. Everybody else seemed to be able to make it work. So why wasn't it working for her?

Maybe, she thought, *if a person messes up as much as I have this last year, she never does amount to anything as a Christian. Maybe I'm not the kind of person God could ever use.*

She thought guiltily about her hopes, before she had left Michigan, to spend lots of time reading her Bible and learning to pray while she was on vacation these two weeks. Instead, she'd gotten so confused by her conversations with MacKenzie and the doubts they produced, as well as her failure with Antonio and Mari, that she'd basically given up trying.

Nikki poked her head into a shop that sold shells, every kind she could imagine, and bought some beautiful ones for her grandparents. She looked into a shop where racks of long dresses of exotic, see-through, tie-dyed material waved gently in the breeze from the open door. There was a crowd of tourists in every store, and on the sidewalks, but in the midst of it all, Nikki felt totally alone. Finally, in the middle of the afternoon, she gave up, bought a magazine then headed back to the hotel.

What you're going to do now, girl, she told her reflection in the rearview mirror of the Grand Am, *is exactly what everybody thinks you've been doing all this time—go lie around the pool and act like this is really a vacation.*

Friday started out like an instant replay of Thursday. The only difference was that Nikki didn't even try shopping. She wrote messages on all the postcards she'd bought the day before, stamped and mailed them, then slathered herself all over with sunscreen and stretched out by the hotel pool.

She lay in the sun, but she couldn't concentrate on her magazine, she didn't feel like swimming, and she was having an awful time trying to shove Ted's words out of her mind. The uneasiness she'd been trying to bury for two days was spoiling everything else. She grabbed her towel and other things, and marched upstairs to her room.

There, she dumped everything unceremoniously on the dresser, grabbed up her Bible, and knelt by the side of her bed.

"Okay, *okay!* I'm here, Lord. I was wrong to stay away from You these last couple of days. It's just that everything is in such a mess, and I feel like such a failure." She opened her Bible to Psalm 9 because Marta had suggested reading the psalm that corresponded to the day's date.

Nikki wasn't at all sure what to expect, but she stopped dead when she reached verse 10: "Those who know your name will trust in you, for you, Lord, have never forsaken those who seek you." *You've never forsaken those who seek you,* her mind repeated. That was an encouraging thought. She got so interested that she took the rest of Marta's advice, which was to add 30 to the date, which meant she'd read Psalm 39 next, then another 30, which put her at Psalm 69, and so on until she read five psalms each day.

When she reached Psalm 69, Nikki felt she'd hit pay dirt. It was about David's problems and how things didn't work out for him all the time, either. But he still ended it with hope, confident that God would always hear.

Does that mean You always hear me, too? she wondered. *How will I know?*

Except for the hum of the air-conditioning, the room remained still. But in that stillness, Nikki could sense that same welcoming presence she'd felt the day she became a Christian. And she could hear in her head the words Marta had told her: *"Sometimes faith can feel like a very risky business."*

Suddenly, the picture of the sandstone bridge that arched from one bluff to the other came into her head, and she felt the same sense of danger she had the morning she'd tried to cross it. Uncomfortably, she realized she had to make a choice between faith and not believing. She struggled for a moment, wondering what she was supposed to do now, then bowed her head.

"I don't know how this is going to turn out, Lord," she prayed, "but I'm making a choice. A choice to trust You."

By 7:30 that night, after a dinner of salad and broiled chicken—since red meat just didn't look very good to her anymore when she remembered the calf's face on MacKenzie's shirt—Nikki was standing in front of the hotel closet, trying to decide which outfit to wear to the party.

On the one hand, she'd felt a little uneasy about going to the party at all. Why had MacKenzie reacted so strongly when Jeremy invited her? Was she getting herself into something she'd regret later?

On the other hand, she thought as she smoothed the soft V-necked teal sweater down over her jeans, *isn't it important to show MacKenzie that I'm not some kind of self-righteous, overly pious type?* MacKenzie had the whole thing wrong, and there was no way Nikki could ever convince her otherwise if they didn't get a chance to talk. Maybe the party would at least give them some common ground.

She tried to park the car in the parking lot by MacKenzie's office building, but the lot was packed full. By the time she found another parking lot—much farther away—and started toward the party, the sky was beginning to darken. Music from the direction of Helton Common was faintly audible in the cool night breeze off the ocean.

Once she reached the large open area, Nikki searched the crowd for MacKenzie's face. *Since she's almost always the tallest girl around,* Nikki thought, *this shouldn't be too difficult.*

But it was. The whole area was one massive crowd of strangers. A few couples danced on the wide-open lawn in the middle, and other people were gathered in groups, lying sprawled on blankets or sitting on short-legged beach chairs they'd brought with them. Nikki saw a couple of people drinking, and it wasn't long before she picked out the smell of marijuana in the evening air.

She watched as several police officers walked the grounds, stopping at one group after another, making people show their identification in what she supposed were age checks, and the comments she overheard about them made her cringe.

One particularly sarcastic comment came from a voice that sounded familiar, and Nikki whirled around to find MacKenzie standing directly behind her.

"Hi, MacKenzie," she began, but the look on MacKenzie's face stopped her dead.

"What are you doing here? Don't tell me, my mother asked you to come, right? To keep an eye on me, maybe? Or did you actually think Jeremy's invitation was serious? Well, when you grow up a little, you'll learn to spot guys like Jeremy. He hits on every girl within the sound of his voice." There were snickers and a few laughs from the group she was with, then MacKenzie turned on her heel and strode away.

Nikki stood there for a minute, hurt and embarrassed, then her brain started to function again.

"MacKenzie!" she shouted.

MacKenzie turned slowly, an annoyed look on her face. "Well?"

Nikki ignored the others standing around MacKenzie and focused only on the taller girl's face. "I'd like to talk to you."

MacKenzie tossed her head so that her sleek russet hair fell back from her forehead, and she gave a long sigh. "Couldn't we do this another time? Like the next time you come in to *help* in the office?" She said the words with such disdain that Nikki flinched, but she could feel the courage building inside her, coming from somewhere she couldn't name.

"No. I really want to talk to you right now."

MacKenzie turned and said something to the others around her that Nikki couldn't quite hear, then turned and walked back to stand in front of Nikki. "Is there a problem here?"

"No," Nikki said, then caught herself. "I mean, yes, there is a problem here. And you know it as well as I do." *I don't really believe you're doing this.* Nikki shook off the negative thought and forced herself to go on. "Can we go someplace where we can talk?" She noted MacKenzie's hesitation and added, "Just for a little while."

MacKenzie shrugged and, turning, led the way across the commons to one of the university buildings. It was far enough away from the band that they could hear each other talk, and when she motioned toward the cement steps, Nikki nodded and sat down, hugging her knees against her chest.

MacKenzie sat down beside her and waited. Nikki swallowed a few times before she began.

"MacKenzie, I think we got off on the wrong foot from the beginning. Maybe because—" she gave a shaky laugh in an attempt to lighten the moment "—your mother tried to force you to spend time with me."

MacKenzie made no response.

Okay! Looks like I'm on my own here, Nikki thought.

"Obviously, I made some big mistakes when I was trying to help out, and I felt terrible about them. So I was knocking myself out to be perfect around you, MacKenzie. I tried to hide some stuff about myself—stuff that happened this past year—so you wouldn't know."

For the first time, Nikki saw a flicker of interest in MacKenzie's face. She went on hurriedly. "See, on Tuesday, when you told me how your mother set this all up so that you'd have to spend time with me, I knew I had to be honest with you. I just didn't want to. You've said things about Christianity that confused me. I'm pretty new at being a Christian, so I wasn't sure how to answer you at first. But I can tell you what happened to me. Almost a year ago, I got pregnant. And the guilt I felt was a lot more than just some 'conditioned response to an archaic thought system,' as you called it. It was real guilt because I really did something wrong."

Nikki swallowed hard and continued. "At first, I almost had an abortion because I didn't want to face the guilt or the consequences of what I'd done. Then my parents tried to force me to have one. And even though I wasn't a Christian yet, I prayed and asked God to help me." Nikki glanced at MacKenzie, who was watching her as she talked. "And He did. He isn't some 'mythical being,' like you said, MacKenzie, because mythical beings can't answer prayers, and He answered mine."

They were both silent for a minute. Nikki stretched out her legs on the cement steps and leaned back, propping her hands behind her.

"After I had Evan—that's my baby's name—it was really hard to give him up for adoption. I got so angry that I almost didn't go through with it, but God came through again. That's when I became a Christian, just a few weeks ago. So like I said, I don't have all the answers yet, but I wanted you to know the truth, MacKenzie—the truth about me, and about God."

Nikki sat silently, hoping for some response, but MacKenzie said nothing. She sat perfectly still, staring out toward the vast Pacific, as if she was no longer even aware that Nikki was there.

Well, I did what I think You were telling me to, God, she thought. *Though it doesn't seem to have done much good.*

Nikki got to her feet. "I'll let you get back to the party now, MacKenzie. Thanks for listening."

MacKenzie glanced at her, then out at the ocean. Nikki started back toward the parking lot. If MacKenzie wouldn't even speak to her, there wasn't much point in hanging around.

She probably thinks I'm crazy for sure now.

As Nikki turned the corner around the first classroom building, the sound of the party behind her became more and more muffled. Soon only a faint strain of music hung in the night air.

She looked up and spotted what she thought was Jupiter shining over the horizon. The campus near the parking lots looked totally deserted, and she realized that everyone not at the party must be at the evening session of Aunt Marta's conference.

Nikki made her way slowly down the sidewalk between the university buildings, walking beside a six-foot-high bank of bougainvillea, breathing in the fresh scent of the ocean. She was so deep in thought about MacKenzie that the sound of voices from the other side of the bushes broke into her consciousness gradually.

She stopped, uneasy, trying to pinpoint the voices.

"Will he do it?"

"I think so."

This second voice was heavily accented, thick.

"I didn't ask for your *opinion*. I asked you, *will he do it?*"

That was the voice of a younger man, lighter in timbre, fluid and polished, and Nikki had the feeling it was someone she knew.

"He will." The heavy voice paused, then added, "I am nearly sure."

The younger voice turned ugly, almost snarling, and Nikki had the fleeting image of whoever it was speaking taking the man with the accent by the throat.

"The one thing I told you was to make sure, absolutely sure, that he is there tonight—that gives you about an hour to make sure he's at the cove."

"Don't worry," the other man broke in with a low, harsh laugh, and he rolled the *r*'s fluently, as though he'd been doing it all his life. "You let me take care of the boy. He is so scared of me, he will do exactly what I tell him to. He is probably already there waiting."

"Right! Look what happened the last time you told me to let you take care of something and not to worry. His father nearly blew the whistle on our whole operation."

"But see how it turned out," the accented voice rushed in. "It took nothing to stop him, less than nothing. One short call to the authorities, and he ran back in Mexico—" there was the sound of fingers snapping "—like that! He knew the police have no love for illegals."

"As you should know."

There was silence for a few seconds, then the accented voice spoke again, a little higher, with a tightness that constricted his words. "I do not know what you are talking about."

The first voice laughed, a harsh laugh that mocked the man he spoke to. "You thought you had me fooled all this time, didn't you? Listen, I'm way ahead of you, and I always will be. Don't you ever forget, I can tell the authorities the same thing against you that you told them against his father. Except in your case, it would be true. Just remember that. And be very sure the boy is there—we need him."

Nikki held her breath, afraid to move for fear of being seen. The voices broke off abruptly, and the footsteps of people striding away in both directions on the other side of the hedge sounded clearly, then began to fade away.

She hesitated a minute, waiting for the men to be gone, when one of the men rounded the corner of the hedge and looked both ways, the long ends of his black mustache evident in the light from the street lamp.

Later, she would realize what a good thing it was that she'd been standing in the shadow of the hedge, so that he did not see her. But at that moment, all she could feel was surprise.

That's Herrera-Ortiz, the one who had a smile on his face when he tore Mari's doll. He was also the one she was sure was forcing Antonio into becoming part of his smuggling operation.

Nikki stood motionless in the shadow of the hedge for several minutes after Herrera-Ortiz disappeared, waiting to see if the other man would appear, too. She had been close, so close, to identifying that other voice until Herrera-Ortiz had appeared. Then the shock of recognizing him had completely driven the other thoughts right out of her mind.

She closed her eyes, trying to bring back the distinctive tone of the other voice, to hear it again while it was still fresh, but it was no use. At last she gave up. It was as maddening as reaching for a word that danced right on the tip of your tongue. You could feel it there, you could almost taste it, but then it turned out to be irretrievable, at least until you were in the middle of something else, like a trig test at school or a heated argument with your parents. Then, at the most inappropriate time, the word you'd been searching for suddenly popped effortlessly into your mind. *Not that it does you any good then,* she thought.

When she was finally convinced that the other man was gone, too, Nikki left the shadows and started down the sidewalk once again.

"His father nearly blew the whistle on the whole operation. . . . It took nothing to stop him, less than nothing. One short call to the authorities . . . " While she'd been listening, the content had not been as important to her as identifying the speakers. But now, it seemed crucial to remember everything she'd just heard.

As she struggled to recall each word, Nikki paused. She thought about Antonio's face, the look she had taken for anger when he said, "If my father could do it, I can, too." How blind could she have been? It hadn't been anger at all, or if it was, it was anger that grew out of the pain of discovering his father was not what he had thought. *"His father nearly blew the whistle on our whole operation. . . . It took nothing to stop him. . . . "*

There was a shock of recognition in her mind, as startling as a splash of ice water. Could it really be Antonio's father they were talking about? She thought through everything she'd heard, both tonight from the men and the other day from Antonio, then tried to add it up a different way to see if she still came out with the same total.

Maybe Antonio doesn't quite have all the information he needs to make this decision, she thought. *And whatever decision it is, he'll have to make it in the next hour.*

❦ Nineteen ❦

NIKKI SLAMMED THE DOOR of the Grand Am, turned the key in the ignition, and took off toward the hotel. Once she got there, she dashed upstairs to the room and kicked off the flimsy sandals she'd worn to the party. She needed her running shoes, sturdy shoes that would carry her down the beach as fast as she could go, and give her feet a firm grip on the boulders she would have to climb.

At night? her thoughts demanded. *You're going to try this in the dark?*

I've been running it nearly every morning. I know the way. Besides, I have no choice. If I don't get there in time, Antonio will get tricked into something that could ruin his life—his and Mari's—forever. I've got try.

She started for the door, then turned back and scrawled a quick note to her aunt on the pad of hotel paper—"Gone to Seal Cove. Back in an hour."

I hope.

Then she grabbed her windbreaker from the closet and

162

pulled the door shut behind her.

When Nikki pulled open the sliding doors that led from the lobby to the beach, a burst of ocean wind jerked her long hair into wild disarray, plastering half of it across her face. She raked the dark strands back from her eyes with shaking fingers as she ran, and pulled a rubber band from the pocket of her jeans without slowing her pace, struggling to tame the thick curls back out of the way.

I can't slow down—can't stop. I have to get there before Herrera-Ortiz does. Antonio has to know. Nikki's lips moved as her feet searched in the dim starlight for the firm sand at the edge of the surf, but whether she murmured the words aloud or only thought them, she wasn't sure. The idea of Antonio stumbling, unaware of what she knew, into Herrera-Ortiz's plan was as loud in her mind as shouting. She had to get to him and tell him what she knew, before it was too late.

The toe of her right running shoe slid across a patch of seaweed lying thick and wet on the shore, and she winced as her ankle twisted briefly underneath her, then caught herself just before she hit the sand.

I'll never make it in the dark, she cried silently. *Oh, Lord, could You at least make the moon come out? Even that much light would help. Just make the fog blow back a little, God, please. How am I supposed to hurry when I keep—?*

"Ouch!" Nikki stumbled as she cracked her toes against the top of a rock embedded in the wet sand.

I'm just trying to help Antonio. And I want to get Mari out of this, safe and sound. Can You help me do that? She's been through so much already.

The thought of Mari spurred her on, and she started off down the beach again. The empty lifeguard hut loomed up out of the dim starlight with a suddenness that startled her. Nikki gasped and veered quickly to the left, thinking at first it was someone standing there. Then she realized what it was, the same deserted hut she ran past every morning, but it seemed to be in a different position somehow.

The crash of the surf sounded louder now, immense and threatening in the darkness, and a shiver ran through her at the realization that she was alone under the dark sky with the vast Pacific roaring at her side. *The wind must be making it sound this way,* she thought. It was a steady, driving wind that blew in off the water like a giant hand trying to push her back, and it was gusting so strongly that it had blown away much of the fog that had shrouded the sky a few minutes earlier. At least there was a brighter glow from the starlight now, and Nikki could make out the bulk of the bluff ahead. Climbing the boulders in the semidarkness would be a challenge, but she was familiar with the way.

She moved toward the first large boulder, the one with the flat top where she could stand and, from there, reach the others she had to climb. Then she stopped, confused. Her eyes had adjusted well enough by now, but somehow she'd lost her bearings.

Oh, Lord, please help me. How am I supposed to do this if I can't even find the right rock? she cried inwardly in frustration. Then she realized what was wrong.

It's high tide. That was why the surf seemed so much louder and things seemed out of place on the beach—the tide was in. The flat-topped rock must be totally covered over at high tide.

She gained access to the path that led up the boulders by veering farther in toward the land and coming at them from the side. But all the time she climbed, a voice kept hammering away in her head, *What about the cavern? If the tide's in, it'll be filled up with water. There's no other way across but the bridge, no other way across but the bridge, no other . . .*

At the back of the cavern was a sheer cliff. There was no way she could go around. All the other times she'd been here it had been low tide and she'd been able to make her way down one side, over the wet, sandy bottom of the empty cavern, then up the far side and on toward the boathouse. But now, with the cavern filled up . . .

Lord, what am I supposed to do? I really need to get to Antonio. You must have had me there tonight at just the right time to hear what Herrera-Ortiz said so that I could get this information to Antonio. And now, well, there's no one else who can help him the way I can right now. So how do You expect me to get to him?

Nikki stopped short at the edge of the bluff. Even in the dim light of the stars, she could see that the cavern was filled with water. Each new wave that washed in sprayed saltwater high into the air beside her. She stood there, gulping in huge breaths of the damp ocean air, then turned and paced a few steps back the way she'd come, trying to keep moving so she wouldn't get a cramp. There, far down the curving coastline, were the lights of Helton Common, dim and misty in the ocean air, and the party she'd just left.

"Okay," she prayed in gasps, still out of breath from running as fast as the light would allow. "I guess this is where I check out, Lord. I tried my best at the party, with MacKenzie, and I struck out." She turned back toward the bridge. "And I tried my best to get to Antonio, and that's not going to work, either. Not unless You have a way to get me across this bridge. I can't do it in the dark."

It was the closest thing she'd ever seen to a miracle, that was for sure. As she stood near the edge of the deep, jagged cavern, the wind blew the last of the fog away, and the crystal-clear face of the nearly full moon shone brightly. Suddenly, there was light enough to see the bridge. There was light enough to cross, if she cared to try.

Nikki didn't know whether to be happy or upset. Happy because the Lord had obviously answered her prayer; upset because the darkness had been the perfect excuse to avoid crossing the bridge. Now the only thing that kept her from crossing was her fear, and there was no way around facing that.

I could go back, she thought wildly. *Run back as fast as I can, get the car, and try to find the old road that Antonio said leads into the boathouse from the highway.* But as soon as she thought it, the absurdity of the idea hit her. If she really thought she could have found the road, she would have gone that way in the first place. She had no idea, not even a hint, where that old road joined the highway.

The only way to help Antonio and Mari in time was to cross the bridge.

She thought how near she'd come to falling that first morning—and how frightening it had been. The minute she'd looked down, the whole world seemed to be moving, and keeping her balance became impossible.

She remembered Ted's words: *"The most important thing is to set your course by something that doesn't move. . . ."*

She glued her eyes to a huge boulder on the far side of the bridge, then took a few deep breaths, very slowly, to calm herself. She stepped out cautiously, reminding herself, *Don't look down. Whatever you do, just don't . . . look . . . down.* She tested each step before she trusted her weight to it.

The ocean rushed underneath her with frightening power. Each time a wave slammed into the sides of the cavern, the bridge trembled a little beneath her feet, and she had to stop and wait until she found the courage to go on. And each time, she had to fight not to look because she knew that one look into that swiftly moving water could throw her off balance and cause her to fall.

She kept her eyes glued on the boulder, which was coming nearer and nearer. "Almost there, you're almost there," she was congratulating herself when an especially strong gust of wind hit her full in the face. Her foot slid and she wobbled, unable to get her balance.

A thrill of fear shot through her as her foot slipped, then caught on a protruding rock. She instinctively threw her arms out to the sides, struggling to balance like a tightrope walker. Then slowly, her heart pounding till she thought it would burst, she found she was able to stand steady again.

Nikki stumbled the last steps across the bridge and hugged the boulder with both arms, shivering, near to tears and trying to catch her breath. When at last her heart stopped pounding double-time, she looked toward the boathouse. It was only a few hundred feet away, and she started for it, hoping Antonio was there and that this wasn't a wild goose chase.

The eucalyptus grove was deserted in the moonlight. Nikki hesitated, wondering what to do next when she heard the sound of a motor growing closer. Far back in the field, behind the grove of eucalyptus trees, she could see parking lights approaching. Her heart began pounding again, harder even than when she'd been crossing the bridge.

She ran to the boathouse, praying the door was unlocked, and pulled at the handle. It opened and she slipped inside, then shut it behind her. In the glow of moonlight from the window, she could see the outline of crates and other equipment stacked along the back wall. Nikki crouched at the end of the row of crates so that she was out of sight. The faint parking lights filled the space outside the window, then the sound of the motor went dead. The door of the boathouse swung open.

In the faint gleam of a flashlight, Antonio appeared in the doorway, then seemed to stumble sideways into the room, Mari whimpering in his arms. Nikki could see a man with a thick mustache over Antonio's shoulder.

Herrera-Ortiz, she thought. Apparently, he had carried out his mission. He pushed Antonio into the boathouse, holding him tight by twisting the T-shirt he wore into a kind of handhold.

"You can just stay in there until the boat comes," he growled. "Until we need you. You don't talk, you don't make any noise at all, hear me?"

The door slammed behind him, and Nikki could hear his footsteps moving away from the boathouse. She heard the squeak of the truck door open, and she crawled out of her hiding place to where Antonio sat on one of the crates.

"Antonio? Mari?"

Antonio gasped, then said something quickly in Spanish.

"It's me. Nikki," she said. "I'm sorry. I didn't mean to scare you."

"What are you doing here?" he whispered, tightening his arms around Mari. In the moonlight, his eyes were dark and frightened, and Mari clutched the doll tightly against her chest with one arm and twisted the other tightly around her brother's neck.

"I had to come, to tell you what I heard."

"No! You don't know what's going on. You have to get out of here before—"

"Shhh!" Nikki hissed. "I *do* know what's going on, at least some of it. And you have to hear it, too." She explained in a rush what she had heard behind the hedge at the party that night. "Antonio, they talked about a man—a father—who almost blew the whistle on their whole operation and how they stopped him by making a call to the authorities and telling them something that wasn't true about him."

Antonio's eyes were wide, and he stared at her intently.

"Well?" she demanded. "Don't you understand?"

Still he stared at her, silent. Then slowly, he started to nod. "That explains the last night, Nikki."

"What last night? What are you talking about?"

"The last night my father was home. He was—upset. He was up all night, pacing the floor, trying to work something out. That morning, he left the house early, in a different direction than he usually went to go to work."

"Do you think he was going to the police?" Nikki asked.

Antonio nodded slowly. "I think maybe he was."

"Antonio! They've tricked you into this whole thing. They got rid of your father because he was turning *them* in, and then they lied to you to keep you quiet."

"And," he added fiercely, shifting Mari's weight on his knees and stroking her head, which sagged sleepily against his chest, "they got me to work for them at the same time! Because I thought . . . " His voice cracked and he looked away from her, his lips tight. "I was not going to come tonight, but Herrera-Ortiz came to the house and forced us into the truck."

"Antonio," she whispered, "you haven't already been involved in the smuggling part, have you?" She held her breath, remembering what Ted had said about the INS being especially tough on anyone involved in drug activities.

"No. They tried, but I have only acted as a guard for them. Usually, they do drops out beyond the islands. But tonight, they are bringing the drugs here. And if you had not told me, I would have helped them this time, to get my father back." He looked up at her and sighed. "They store the drugs here, in this shed, until they can get them to Los Angeles and other cities. That is why I was here so much, to guard the drugs in the boathouse. I am sorry for lying to you, Nikki."

But Nikki hardly heard his apology. "What do you mean, 'do drops'?"

"They drop the drugs from a boat or a small plane. Usually they weight the bales of drugs and sink them in the water, out beyond the islands. Then they send divers out to get them later. But I heard Herrera-Ortiz say there are too many patrol boats by the islands now—someone tipped off the coast guard. When that happens, they bring the drugs here to the cove, on a small boat, very late at night."

Nikki was still processing the first part of his statement. "They just drop them in the *water?*"

"Wrapped in plastic."

"And it doesn't damage—?" She broke off and scurried back to her hiding place at the sound of footsteps approaching.

Herrera-Ortiz pulled open the door and shone his flashlight inside. He flashed it across Antonio's face and made a small, derisive sound with his mouth. He said something rough and short in Spanish, then turned to go. Then Nikki froze in horror as Antonio spoke. In a clear, quiet voice, she heard him saying, "I will not help you anymore."

The older man swung around instantly. "*What?*" he barked.

"I said, I will not help you anymore."

Not now, Antonio! Nikki thought. *Not now! Not like this.* She held her breath.

Herrera-Ortiz pushed the door open all the way and strode to Antonio's side, shouting a torrent of Spanish words that were completely unintelligible to Nikki. But the sense of menace on his dark face needed no translating. Nikki cowered further back behind the crate.

Then Herrera-Ortiz stopped dead. He straightened up and seemed to get control of himself. He reached into his jacket, pulled out a small handgun, and pointed it not at Antonio, but directly at the head of Mari, who was by now sound asleep. Then he spoke in a carefully controlled voice, in English once again.

"I think you will change your mind. Hear me. Including you, I have exactly the right number of men coming tonight to help unload the boat. If we are one person short, it will make the work much longer and increase our chances of being found out. And then *my* boss will not be happy."

Nikki's mouth was dry with fear. She remembered the man's ruthlessness when he tore the dress on Mari's doll, and thought about what he had done to Antonio's father. What would he do to Antonio if he didn't go along with him? Had she made things worse by coming?

Herrera-Ortiz started back outside, then turned deliberately. "I will call you when the boat arrives. You *will* come." His footsteps moved away again, but Nikki stayed where she was, frantically trying to think what she should do.

She tried to guess the time. She thought back to the party, to her breathless run down the dark beach and over the bridge, and estimated it must be about 9:30. Aunt Marta might not arrive back at the hotel room for hours, especially if she went out with friends for coffee after the evening session. Then she'd wonder where on earth Nikki was. But it wouldn't be soon enough.

Nikki could hear other voices outside with Herrera-Ortiz now and realized that once they started unloading the boat and loading the drugs into the boathouse, there would be no way for her to hide. She started to pray, not just for herself, but also for Antonio and Mari, that God would send help.

Herrera-Ortiz was striding back and forth outside, and when he reached a certain point in each rotation, she could see him through the boathouse window, a radio receiver to his ear.

Across the room, Antonio was whispering. "I have been a fool. They tricked me all along, and I understand now they have been lying about helping bring my father back, too. They would never bring back someone who would inform the police what they are doing." The sadness and desperation in his voice chilled her. She searched for words to say but found none. Then there was noise outside again.

The door swung open, and Herrera-Ortiz put his head inside. "The boat is here. Come."

Antonio laid Mari on the cold floor and took off his denim jacket and covered her gently. Then he followed Herrera-Ortiz.

Nikki gave them a few seconds to get away from the boathouse, then hurried to the window. She could faintly see the stairs they were taking down the cliff to the water, and she could watch them on the beach and the small dock. There was a long conversation once they reached the sand, with Herrera-Ortiz gesturing as he gave them instructions. Then the men—she counted five of them in the beam of a flashlight—went to work in silence, with hurried, furtive glances back up at the cliffs.

They began unpacking two black inflatable boats and a large coil of rope. They set up a small compressor, snapped the end of the hose over the valve, and began to pump the boats full of air. When the boats were full, they packed away the compressor and anchored the rope to a boulder. Then they waited silently.

What are they waiting for? Nikki wondered and shivered in the damp night air. *How much longer will this take?* She realized how much colder it had become, and she turned and laid her windbreaker over Antonio's jacket, tucking them both in around the sleeping child. She turned and again stared out the window.

Then Herrera-Ortiz pointed, and Nikki looked out toward the surf. The boat they were waiting for must be here, but she couldn't see a thing in the black water.

❧ *Twenty* ❧

IT TOOK A FEW MINUTES of staring before Nikki could make out what the men were pointing at. Far out in the water, a small white light blinked on and off, swaying with the motion of the waves. It came closer and closer, then stopped, she thought, although it was difficult to judge either motion or distance now that the wind had stopped and the air was turning misty once again.

Two men grabbed the coil of rope, climbed into one of the inflatable boats, and started off toward the blinking light, playing out the rope as they went. On shore, Herrera-Ortiz hurried to Antonio and pushed him forward.

"Go!" he said brusquely, jerking his head toward the second inflatable where another man from the truck waited.

When the first inflatable reached the blinking light, a brighter, steady light came on, illuminating a sailboat that rocked gently beyond the surf where the swells began. The ship had a ghostly look to it, riding the waves so silently. Nikki could see now that the blinking light she had noticed first was fastened to the masthead and that the boat was much closer to shore than she had estimated. Men on board grabbed the rope and tied it to something on the boat, and after that it was simple work for the men in the inflatables to haul themselves from ship to shore and back.

Shadows crossed back and forth in front of the ship's powerful light, and Nikki could see large bales being eased into the first inflatable boat. When it was full, they pulled it back to shore, and as soon as one of the men jumped out and hauled the boat safely up onto the sand, Herrera-Ortiz gestured with his gun.

"Now," he ordered, and the second boat followed the path the first had taken, Antonio's hands grabbing over and over on the rope to propel them toward the light.

On shore, the fourth and fifth men were hoisting the hay-bale-size loads to their backs, then struggling up the steps to the cliff above. Nikki knew that her safety in the boathouse was over. She turned away from the window and bent down to give Mari's hair one last gentle pat, then slipped out the door and around to the back of the building. At least that way, she would be close enough to hear if Mari woke and cried out. From around the front of the building came the sound of the sliding door on the truck being opened and a *thump*, then each man returned to the beach for another bale.

Over and over the process was repeated, the first few bales going into the truck, the rest stacked up in the boathouse. The inflatables went out empty, came in full, and were emptied again. Nikki had no idea of the price of marijuana, but it was obvious that a great deal of money was changing hands tonight. The men were evidently well-organized and trained, and she could see why Antonio was so important in Herrera-Ortiz's plan.

By that time, Nikki's hair was damp to the scalp from the foggy ocean wind, and she'd lost track of time. She felt that she'd been hiding there behind the boathouse for hours, but there was no way to get back to the hotel without crossing the bluff and the sandstone bridge in full view of the men. She worried wearily what Aunt Marta was thinking about her absence but pushed the thought away since there was nothing she could do about it. She could see Herrera-Ortiz still alternately issuing whispered orders and holding the radio receiver to his ear.

He's getting instructions from someone else, she thought and tried again to decipher who it was that had spoken to him behind the hedge. *I'm sure I know that voice.*

Bales were stacked high on the beach now—she estimated 50 or more—and the men lugging them up the cliff path to the boathouse were moving slower, apparently getting tired from the exhausting work. Herrera-Ortiz must have seen it, too, because the next time Antonio's inflatable boat worked its way to shore, he waved his arm at them, motioning them to leave their boat on shore and become part of the carrying crew.

With Antonio working, the bales disappeared more quickly up the cliff to the boathouse. The work light from the larger boat blinked four times, and Nikki heard Herrera-Ortiz's radio crackle, then spring into life. He listened, then put it to his mouth and spoke. Then he lifted his flashlight and gave one long wave, and the light on the boat went out.

Can this finally be over? Nikki wondered. And what would happen to Antonio and Mari now? And to her, if they caught her? *Lord, are You going to just let Herrera-Ortiz and the others get away?*

The second inflatable boat brought in the last bales to shore, and Nikki held her breath. There was a minute then when the men from the truck and Antonio and Herrera-Ortiz were all on the beach together. Herrera-Ortiz handed something to each of them—except Antonio—and they turned to start back up the cliff to the truck.

Suddenly, in a burst of light so brilliant that Nikki automatically squeezed her eyelids shut, the entire beach was illuminated as though it were noon. She heard a loud hissing that sounded like fireworks on the Fourth of July, and when she opened one eye and squinted at the sky, she could see that a whole volley of flares had been shot off. Before the glare of them was completely gone, a helicopter glided into place overhead, its spotlights aimed directly down at the beach.

The men on the beach stood stock-still, staring at the sky, as though frozen in place. Loudspeakers began to blare.

"THIS IS THE POLICE. WE HAVE YOU SURROUNDED. DO NOT TRY TO RUN. THERE IS NO CHANCE TO GET AWAY."

As if in response, three of the men took off down the beach, two raced up the cliff steps, and Herrera-Ortiz, to Nikki's amazement, turned and rushed into the surf with high steps through the shallows, then paddled in the deeper water with all his might. Nikki thought that, in his panic, he must not have seen the speedboat that seemed to hydroplane directly at the sailboat that had delivered the bales.

It was no use, though. Before any of the men had gotten far, the officers were on them with handcuffs and drawn guns. It seemed to Nikki that the police had materialized out of thin air, though she realized they must have been hidden close by. Within 10 minutes, all the men from the truck were back on the beach, handcuffed, beside Antonio, who had remained motionless the whole time. A dripping-wet policeman, his expression disgusted, led a thoroughly soaked Herrera-Ortiz from the water to stand by the other men.

Another officer began herding all the prisoners toward the speedboat that had been tied up beside the dock. To her dismay, Nikki saw that Antonio was also in handcuffs. The unfairness of it overwhelmed her, and she rushed out from behind the boathouse, past the truck, and down the stairs.

"Wait a minute!" she yelled. She tried to sprint toward the prisoners but found herself moving almost in slow motion through the thick sand. Some officers rushed toward her, alarmed, and she stopped and held her hands out in front of her. "You can't take him—not that one!" They stared at her as she pointed at Antonio. "They *made* him come. He didn't want to. That man—" she nodded at Herrera-Ortiz "—had a gun pointed at him all night. You can't arrest Antonio!"

"Sorry, miss. We have no evidence of force being used to get any of these men involved," one of the officers replied.

"But the *gun*—what about the *gun* Herrera-Ortiz had?" she cried.

"We found no sign of any gun."

"He must have tossed it in the water," she told him. "That's why he jumped in, so you wouldn't see him dump the gun in there."

Nikki was feeling quite pleased with herself for figuring that out when she realized that the officers weren't at all impressed. Instead, the tallest of them came closer. "Who exactly are you, miss, and what are you doing out here?"

Until that instant, Nikki hadn't thought how her being there must look to the police. She opened her mouth to answer, but words wouldn't come. Instead, she began to shake all over.

"Well?" the officer demanded, but still she could not speak.

There was a commotion on the dock, and Nikki glanced beyond the officer to see several people getting off the speedboat. She did a double-take, then asked, "Aunt Marta? Ted? What are *they* doing here?" She thought she'd never been so glad to see anybody before. Behind them came Alex and MacKenzie. Everything got very confused then, with Ted wrapping his jacket around a shivering Nikki, and Aunt Marta hugging her close.

"What's going on?" Nikki kept asking. "What are you doing here?" Then she turned to Ted. "They arrested Antonio! He's the one I told you about, and they *tricked* him into this. Herrera-Ortiz—the one with the mustache—he had a gun and *made* him do it. He *made* Antonio unload the drugs. Please, you have to explain to the police—you have to *do* something!"

Ted squeezed her shoulder and nodded. "Don't worry. The drug agents have been watching the whole time, and I think they'll give plenty of evidence in Antonio's favor." He walked toward the prisoners.

Nikki sighed and turned back to her aunt, who gave her a wry grin before she spoke. "And here all this time I thought you were just sitting by the pool and jogging on the beach! I can't wait to hear how all this came about."

Nikki winced. "Aunt Marta, I wasn't trying to hide anything from you. I tried to tell you about all of this the other night, but you were so busy."

Marta hugged Nikki briefly. "Next time, would you mind warning me when you're about to give me life-and-death-type information? I'll be sure to put aside my work then!"

She saw Nikki's eye fill with tears, and she dropped her

teasing tone immediately. "Nik, I'm just kidding. Listen, I'll hear the whole story, and we'll get everything worked out as soon as we get back to the hotel, okay?"

"I'm sorry," Nikki said. "I don't mean to get upset. It's just that I had such big plans for this vacation, and everything that could possibly go wrong *has*. I just wanted to be like you and Jeff and Ted—all these Christians that have it all together. But everything I touched seemed to get messed up." She stopped and brushed away tears with both her hands. "Anyway, you're right. We can talk about this later. But how did you all get here so fast? The police just—"

Alex and MacKenzie, who had hung back a few steps while Nikki and Marta talked privately, moved closer. "We've been here a long time, at least a couple of hours," Alex said.

"*What?*"

"That's right," Marta agreed. "The SWAT team was deployed here before the drug boat even came in, and when we told the police that you were involved somehow, they let us come with them on the coast guard boat."

"But why? I mean, how did you know—?" Nikki asked.

MacKenzie spoke then, and her voice was kinder than Nikki had ever heard it. "After you left the party, I couldn't stop thinking about what you told me, Nikki. I think it must have cost you a lot to be honest with me like that. I called your hotel room, but you weren't there, so I found your aunt at the end of the conference session to see if maybe you were with her."

Marta took up the story. "Then *I* called the room, and you weren't there. I checked with the desk and the restaurant, and nobody could find you. It was about 10:00 by then, so I was getting very concerned. Alex and MacKenzie and I went back to the hotel to look for you and we found your note. At that point, I called Ted." She nodded toward Ted, who was back now, standing beside her.

"I'm sorry, Nikki," he put in. "I had to tell them about our conversation in the restaurant, about you meeting illegals and all that. But the thing that really clinched it for me was when you insisted we sail closer to this cove while we were sailing the other day. When we got close enough, I could see that the dock and the steps had been repaired here. I'm up and down this coastline a lot, and I knew this dock had been pretty much wrecked in the storms that ruined the house. That really got me thinking. Then when I saw your note, I put it all together." He shrugged. "I called the coast guard and the local police. Turns out they've known for some time that a big drop was to be made tonight. They just didn't know where . . . until we showed them your note and told them—"

There was a shout from the dock then, and they all swung around toward the sound. "Nikki! Nikki!" It was Antonio's voice. The officer had his hand on Antonio's back, guiding him down the step and into the low overhang of the cabin doorway. Just before he disappeared, he shouted, "Mari! Get Mari!"

"I will!" she shouted back over the noise of the surf and turned and started swiftly back up the steps. "Good grief, I can't believe I forgot all about Mari!"

The others followed her to the boathouse.

"Come on, I'll show you," she answered.

She ran into the boathouse, then stopped with a sigh of relief. Mari was still asleep, just as Nikki had left her, now surrounded on three sides by the neatly stacked bales. Nikki gently picked up the child and explained to the others who she was. Two officers had followed the group up the stairs, and they took Mari from her.

Despite their assurances that the child would be well cared for, Nikki's eyes filled with tears at the thought of the tiny girl waking up in a strange place without anyone she knew around her. She tucked Mari's doll securely under the child's arm and prayed that somehow, some way, God would bring the right people along to provide a safe place for Mari during what was sure to be a scary time.

Nikki was so weary that she could barely stay on her feet, but in this night of surprises, there was one more surprise she could never have imagined. The helicopter, which had been hovering overhead the entire time, moved in closer than ever and directed its spotlight at a tree-covered spot on one of the cliffs a little farther down the beach. Several officers were running toward the trees and surrounding them. The helicopter came in so close that the small, brushy trees lay down nearly flat, and the officers dove in and pulled out a man hidden there.

Nikki hurried with the others up the path and watched as the man was half dragged, half carried to one of the squad cars parked behind the eucalyptus grove. Nikki craned her neck to see, then drew back in shock when she realized that this was the first time she'd ever seen Professor Lee Tierney look foolish. In his usual chinos and denim shirt, he bowed his head as an officer pushed down on his dark, curly hair and made sure the professor didn't bump his head getting into the car. Nikki realized then why she had recognized that other voice behind the hedge, the one that had threatened Herrera-Ortiz.

Ted cleared his throat, then said quietly, "Well, that

pretty much wraps things up. The one thing the agents were disappointed about was that they didn't get the man who masterminded the entire operation. So I guess this will make their night."

Nikki threw a quick glance at MacKenzie, whose face was a study in disbelief and anger.

"They're making a terrible mistake! Lee would never, *ever* be involved in something like this! I don't believe it," she kept saying, shaking her head over and over. She started toward the squad car as though she couldn't help herself. For once, her perfect dancer's posture abandoned her, and her shoulders slumped forward.

MacKenzie had been so sure, so confident, so *right* about everything—or so Nikki had thought. And now, right in front of her eyes, it was all being destroyed. Nikki couldn't help aching for her.

Marta was almost as dumbfounded as MacKenzie had been. "I can hardly believe it, either," she said. "Lee Tierney? He's been on faculty here for years, hasn't he, Alex? How could he have been involved in drug smuggling all this time without anyone knowing it?"

"No one knew, Marta," Alex said sadly, "but some of us have suspected for a long time. He was simply too smart to ever pin anything on. The agents told me they had noticed a direct correlation between the parties he encouraged at Helton Common—parties that usually drew the police because of the drugs and alcohol involved—and the biggest drug operations. It was almost as though they were purposely created as a diversion. But they could never get the proof they needed."

"Well, this time they caught him red-handed," one of the

agents who was standing with them added. "He was hiding up there in the trees the whole time, directing the entire operation by radio."

Five days later, Nikki sat on the edge of the pool, swinging her legs back and forth absently in the cool water and watching as the sun glinted off its surface. She listened intently while MacKenzie, perched beside her on the gray cement, spoke.

"It was one shock on top of another," MacKenzie said, her knees drawn up to her chest and her arms around them. "I always had this idea that Christians were totally self-righteous, you know? Like they thought they were better than everybody else. And then you went and started telling me about all the mistakes you'd made." She looked up quickly. "Don't get the idea I've changed my mind or anything! But it did kind of blow me away."

She ran her thumb back and forth over the perfectly polished pink nail of her big toe as she went on. "And then this whole thing with Lee . . ."

She broke off, and they sat in silence for a few minutes until MacKenzie could talk again. "Just about everybody on campus thought he was the coolest professor. And when he started paying special attention to me—asking me to be his assistant and all—I thought I was the luckiest person in the world. Now I know he was using me the whole time, the way he used everybody. Even that boy—Antonio. Here I thought it showed what a nice guy he was, the way he'd help 'disadvantaged' kids, but he was doing it so he could get them involved in his smuggling operation." She shook her head. "I thought he was so smart, about legalizing drugs and about the whole environmental thing, and it was all just a cover for his own greed." She turned to look at Nikki. "Did you read that article about him in the Sunday paper?"

Nikki shook her head, waiting.

"It said he paid cash for his Porsche—drug money." She rolled her eyes. "I knew he paid cash, all right. But he told me it was money he'd *inherited*. Now that I know what was really going on, I can see how he played me for a fool. He was always asking me to grade papers for him and stuff because he was so busy going to all these conferences." MacKenzie's voice turned bitter. "Conferences, my foot! He was setting up drug deals with his suppliers in other countries. Anyway, that's enough about Lee Tierney. I don't even want to *think* about him anymore, except that I hope they give him the longest jail sentence possible!" MacKenzie slid off the side of the pool and into the water, which reached just above her waist, and swung her arms around in half circles, watching the sun create a pattern of diamonds on the surface.

Nikki watched her silently. It was almost as though she actually wanted to talk to Nikki now, whereas before, she'd done everything possible to avoid it.

"What's happening to Antonio and his sister now?"

Nikki smiled. "Mari ended up with a foster family that's part of Ted's church, and I've been able to go and see her every day. And they released Antonio yesterday into Ted's custody. He'll still have to go before the judge, but Ted says the whole thing about 'extenuating circumstances' will help him a lot. The police got a statement out of Herrera-Ortiz that he'd lied about Antonio's father, too, so they think the judge will rule that he can come back to the States soon, since Ted's church is willing to sponsor the whole family. That way, they can *all* become citizens, not just Mari."

Nikki put her hands on the pavement behind her and leaned back. "I didn't see how things could ever work out for them, but I guess they are."

"Thanks to Ted," MacKenzie put in.

Nikki grinned, remembering what she'd thought of Ted the first time she'd seen him. "Yeah, Ted turned out to be an all-right guy."

MacKenzie shook her head back and forth. "Well, he's certainly not much to look at, but your aunt doesn't seem to mind."

Nikki had to agree with that. Since the night of Lee's arrest, Marta seemed to be seeing her old friend through new eyes.

And Ted was doing his part. Nikki had to laugh, remembering how he'd winked at her after church that past Sunday, pushing out his new tie with one thumb for her inspection. "I think it's working, Nik," he'd said. "How about we go pick out another one? For when I take Marta out to dinner before you two leave?"

"Well, he's certainly persuasive," MacKenzie was saying. "He's after me to go to this group that meets on campus— something called InterVarsity."

"Oh, I hope you will, MacKenzie!" Nikki said.

In answer, MacKenzie shrugged, then stretched her arms out in front of her and slid underneath the shining water. Nikki watched her, and a prayer went up automatically from her heart for this girl who had become a friend.

❧ Epilogue ❧

Callen@aol.com

Hi, Carly! Hi, Jeff!

Sorry I haven't answered your last E-mail. I really have been busy—and don't laugh! I'm not talking about doing the pool and beach thing. I'm doing that now, but I sure wasn't last week.

You might say I got a little bit more than the vacation I bargained for when I came along to Santa Linnea. I won't be able to explain it all until I get back, but I can tell you this. MacKenzie's thinking about going to an InterVarsity group here at South State. If somebody told me last week this time that she'd be doing that, I'd have laughed out loud.

And remember the guy I told you about? Antonio? You won't believe what's going on with him and his little sister. Anyway, we're leaving tomorrow morning, so I'll tell you all about it when we get back.

Talk to you soon,
Nikki

P.S. You'll even get to meet Ted. Aunt Marta invited him to spend a week with us at Lake Michigan this summer. Sounds like serious stuff to me!

Nikki clicked on *Send* and, while she waited for the "Mail has been sent" message, leaned back in her chair and thought about all that had happened in the last two weeks. Everything *was* different, now that she was a Christian, but not in the ways she'd expected. She still messed things up. Her past was still her past. But she'd taken a few first baby steps in faith, and she was learning that God was there, and she could depend on Him.